Holly's Wishes

Book Two: Whispered Wishes Series

Karen Pokras

Grand Daisy Press

Grand Daisy Press
PO Box 30241
Elkins Park, PA 19027

Publisher's Note: This is a work of fiction. Names, characters, places, and incidents are a product of the author's imagination. Locales and public names are sometimes used for atmospheric purposes. Any resemblance to actual people, living or dead, or to businesses, companies, events, institutions, or locales is completely coincidental.

Edited by Melissa Ringsted of There For You Editing
Cover by Najla Qamber Designs
Models: Courtney Boyett and Willis Totten
Model Photographer: Casey Boyett
Book Layout ©2013 BookDesignTemplates.com

Holly's Wishes/Karen Pokras. -- 1st ed.
ISBN 978-0-9962843-1-8

For more information, please visit
www.karenpokras.com

"Ultimately, we wish the joy of perfect union with the person we love."

−Mortimer Adler

The Whispered Wishes Series

Ava's Wishes
Holly's Wishes
Tessa's Wishes
Woven Wishes
Merry Wishes: An E-book Novella

Five Years Later

"I still don't get why she chose you to be the maid of honor," Tessa whined, adjusting the straps of her lavender silk gown for the hundredth time.

"We've already been over this," Holly replied, twisting around in front of the mirror to pin up a strand of long blonde hair that had already escaped the hairdresser's elaborate up-do. "It's an age thing. I'm only two years younger than Ava. You're six years younger. Don't take this the wrong way, but she still thinks of you as a little kid."

"But I'm twenty-one," she reminded her older sister. "I'm hardly a child. I'm practically the same age Ava and Max were when they met and got engaged."

"I remember it well," Holly said, smiling.

Ava met Max during their senior year of college. To say their relationship started off awkward was an understatement. He had been a nude model in her art class, who, oddly enough, wound up being her statistics tutor. They'd been like oil and water at first, but they shared a bond that kept pulling them together. They fell in love and were engaged within a matter of weeks. Holly couldn't help but feel a little jealous. She was happy for them, of course, but jealous nonetheless.

"Being a bridesmaid is a huge honor. You shouldn't be complaining. You still get to stand up there with us in your glamorous gown."

Tessa twirled in the mirror. "Well, I do look good, there's no arguing there."

Holly rolled her eyes. "Anyway, choosing the wedding party wasn't my decision. It was Ava's. I had nothing to do with it." Picking up the can of hairspray, she added enough of the sticky goo to her head to ensure no other strays would escape, before moving on to makeup. Why bother hiring professionals if she was just going to have to touch everything up herself?

"In that case, I'm officially putting in my application to be your maid of honor. You're going to be next, you know. It seems like you and Jared have been together forever." Tessa took a seat at the vanity next to her sister and rummaged through the makeup pile to find the eye shadow that matched her dress.

She added extra color to her already perfectly done eyes before moving on to lips.

Holly nodded. It did seem like she and Jared had been together forever. In reality, it had been three years. She'd first noticed him back when they were still in college and living in the same dorm. The attraction had been instant—at least for her. Despite the fact that they were and would always be complete opposites, she'd fallen hard. Normally, she stuck to *nice guys*, the type of guys her parents would expect her to date. Not that Jared wasn't *nice*—he just had a bit of a wild side that Holly found fascinating. No, that wasn't the right word ... *sexy*, that's what it was. When it came down to it, he was sexy, and she'd never dated anyone like that before.

For months, she tried pretty much everything to catch his attention, but he hadn't noticed her. Not at first. Not for a long time, actually. He was too busy partying to be bothered with a dean's list girl, which probably explained why he eventually dropped out of school. Holly had been bummed at first, but went back to dating the kind of guys she could proudly bring home—nice, college educated, *boring* guys.

The following year, she walked into a friend's party and recognized him immediately. She offered him a drink and struck up a conversation. Within six months, they moved in together. They'd been playing house ever since. Despite countless hints that it might be time to take their relationship to the next level, she was still waiting on a marriage proposal.

"Duly noted," Holly said, although, in the event that she and Jared ever did get married, she couldn't imagine anyone but Ava as her matron of honor. Poor Tessa. It couldn't be easy being the youngest sister.

The door to the bridesmaids' room slowly creaked open.

"There she is!" Holly exclaimed, turning in her chair to face the youngest member of the bridal party. "The prettiest flower girl I've ever seen." She opened her arms to scoop Jenna up and hold her close.

"Aunt Holly! You're smooshing my dress," Jenna complained, wiggling her tiny body free. "Watch me …"

The little girl put her basket of flower petals down and spun around in circles, squealing in delight as the skirt of her dress flared out like a ballerina's tutu.

"Just beautiful," Holly proclaimed, clapping her hands in delight. "The most beautiful three-year-old there ever was."

"Almost four," Jenna stated in a very serious tone.

"Yes, of course you are," Ava said, as she entered the room. "My daughter loves to remind everyone her birthday is soon."

Holly barely recognized her older sister in her wedding gown. She couldn't help but stare. Ava was glowing. The old cliché that a bride looks like a princess really was true. She looked as if she'd stepped out of a Disney movie, and other than the birth of her daughter, she'd never appeared happier.

She was finally getting the big white wedding she and Max had decided to put off for a few years. There'd always seemed to be something standing in the way. Not that the birth of Jenna was just a *something,* but Ava's pregnancy had been unexpected and difficult. At the same time, they had school to finish and careers to get off the ground. Now that their lives were a bit more stable, they'd decided it was time to have the wedding of their dreams. Well, Ava's dreams really. Max seemed content with the marriage certificate the Justice of the Peace issued them almost five years ago, shortly after they'd moved to California and learned they had a baby on the way.

"Oh ..." Holly sighed, standing up to take her sister's hands, "you're absolutely stunning."

"Breathtaking," Tessa added, breaking into the circle. It had been a long time since the three of them had been together like this.

"Stop it, now," Ava said, her cheeks turning pink, "both of you. You're going to make me cry. I've waited way too long for this day to have my makeup ruined five minutes before I'm about to walk down the aisle."

While Holly dabbed Ava's eyes with the edge of a tissue, Tessa retied the bow on Jenna's lavender dress, a miniature version of the ones she and Holly wore. Each of the women picked up their flowers and stood together before the mirror … three sisters, bonded by blood, the best of friends.

"Hey, I want to see, too," Jenna said, squeezing between Ava and Holly.

A sea of lavender surrounded Ava's white satin and silk gown, matching the bouquet of lilacs and daisies each of them carried. The Haines ladies were a sight to behold today.

A knock on the door interrupted the moment.

"Yes?" Holly called out.

"They're ready for you now," the voice on the other side said.

A va's ceremony had everything Holly had always dreamed of for herself. Well, the most important thing anyway—the adoring groom waiting at the altar, unable to take his eyes off his bride from the moment she walked into the room. Not that she was in love with Max. She had Jared. She knew Jared loved her, but did he adore her? It seemed as if they'd hit a wall recently ... or maybe that wall had always been there, and she'd chosen not to see it. Either way, she hoped a marriage certificate would be just the thing they needed to break through and forge ahead into a blissfully happy future.

It felt like everyone around Holly was getting married lately. Of course, she was twenty-five now, and she and her friends were at that age. She'd thought maybe once Jared's friends started marrying, he might decide he wanted to as well, but he appeared more than content in his current single state. Her mom had warned her against moving in with him for that very reason. Why did she always have to be right?

With the ceremony now over and the reception in full swing, she watched as her boyfriend stood at the bar ordering a drink. Was this his third or his fourth? She'd lost count.

"Who's that talking to Jared?" Tessa asked, coming up behind her.

"That's Carly, one of Ava's friends from college. I didn't know they were still friends. I thought Ava told me they'd lost touch after she moved out west. I guess they reconnected."

"Interesting outfit," Tessa noted, eyeing the barely there dress with disdain.

Holly nodded. "She looks like she belongs on a corner."

"Well, she certainly doesn't look like she came from church. Whoever was sitting behind her sure got an eyeful every time she knelt, that's for sure."

They bowed their heads and giggled, trying not to draw any attention their way.

"How does she know Jared?" Tessa asked once she calmed herself down.

"She doesn't." Holly turned her attention back to her boyfriend, watching as he flirted shamelessly with her. "They've never met before today," she said, sighing.

"Oh, forget about them. He's being annoying … and harmless. Besides, this is an awesome party, isn't it? Hey, I love this song. Come on, let's dance!" Without giving her a chance to respond, Tessa pulled her out onto the center of the floor.

Holly could always count on her younger sister to lighten the mood. It was as if she could sense what she was feeling. Maybe it was a sister thing. Whatever it was, dancing with Tessa did cheer her up. This was Ava's wedding. It wasn't the time or the place for being irritated. She would deal with Jared and his inappropriate behavior later.

"Ooh, I almost forgot—I'll be back in a minute," Holly said, breaking away during the second song. She hurried up on stage to whisper in the ear of the lead singer of the band and returned to Tessa, smiling, as she waited for the music to end.

Moments later, the singer announced, "May I have everyone's attention please? The Maid of Honor would like to toast the happy couple."

He waited for Holly to grab her champagne before handing over the microphone. The wait staff quickly made their rounds, refilling everyone's glasses. Ava and Max took their drinks and sat down at the head table.

Looking at her sister and brother-in-law, Holly started, "Ava, Max ... this is kind of a strange toast for me to make. Not strange as in weird, but strange as in different. I've never made a wedding toast before to a couple who weren't actually newlyweds." She scanned the room before asking, "I'm allowed to say that, right? It wasn't a big secret that the two of you have already been married for almost five years?"

The two of them nodded as the room burst out laughing.

"Phew, that would have been really uncomfortable for all of us if I'd let that little secret out," Holly continued. "But, since we're all good, as I was saying, normally in these kinds of speeches, the sister of the bride welcomes the groom into her family. However, Max, you've been a part of our family for a while. I'm thrilled we haven't scared you away." Pausing, she waited while everyone's chuckles ended. "I'll never forget the day we met. You sat at our family's kitchen table in front of all of us—Mom, Dad, Tessa, and myself—while Ava slept on the couch. You know she broke the cardinal rule, don't you? She left the boyfriend alone with the family on the first meeting. That was a big no-no."

Max laughed along with Ava and everyone else.

"Luckily, you handled yourself like a champ," she continued. "You even managed to convince Mom and Dad to allow my sister to move across the country with you after only knowing her a few weeks. That, my friend, was a bold move … very impressive. Of course, I don't think they expected you to knock her up after a couple of months, but we won't discuss that. Oops."

She blew Ava a kiss, who stuck her tongue out in return. Jenna may have been unplanned, but she was one of the most adored members of the family. She was also currently fast asleep in a side room with a babysitter; otherwise, Holly never would have brought up the subject so crudely.

"Ava, when you first called me to tell me about Max, you didn't exactly sound head over heels. In fact, it was sort of the opposite. I'm not going to go into the specifics of how you first met. I'm not sure it's appropriate to give Dad a heart attack at your wedding, or embarrass you further in front of your guests." With a wink, she mouthed the words, "Tell you later, Dad." Holly glanced back over to Ava and Max. "However, I will say that when you two did come to your senses … you fell hard and fast. In fact, I can honestly say, I've never witnessed a love quite like the one between the two of you before." She peeked toward the bar where Jared was talking to yet another scantily clad woman and made a mental note to talk to Ava about her friends' clothing choices. "Now, five years later, that love is as strong as ever, and I couldn't be happier for the two of you. Ava, Max, I wish you both a lifetime of love and happiness. Max, welcome to the family … again."

Raising her glass, Holly took a sip of her champagne, and handed the microphone back to the singer. As she walked over to hug her sister and brother-in-law, she spotted someone at the edge of the room. *Could it be?*

Holly strained her eyes trying to figure out if it was really *him*. She couldn't be a hundred percent sure. She hadn't seen him since high school. It certainly *looked* like him, but if it was, what was he doing here? She knew he wasn't one of Ava's friends. At least she didn't think he was. Unless ... did they go to college together? She supposed it was possible. Or maybe Max knew him, but Max wasn't even from Forest Hills. His family lived almost four hours away.

Oh hell, Holly. If you don't go over there you'll never know. She took small sips of her drink as she gathered the courage to approach him. He was sitting alone, typing on his phone.

"Hol." Jared grabbed her arm as she'd started to walk toward the mystery man. Swinging her around, he nearly spilled champagne all over her gown. "Come dance with me, baby. We never dance anymore, and you look so hot tonight." He dragged her toward the band.

"You're drunk," she replied matter-of-factly, tugging back. The last thing she wanted to do was make a fool of herself in front of this crowd with her sloshed boyfriend.

"I'm only a little buzzed. Have some fun with your old man." He was stronger and determined, and she reluctantly let him pull her onto the dance floor.

She glanced over to where *he* was sitting, but his chair was now empty. *Shoot.* She tried to back up as Jared flung himself around in a series of embarrassing moves resembling something out of a seventies disco flick. Before she could get out of the way, he grabbed her wrist, yanking her into *Saturday Night Hell.* His attempt at twirling her around resulted in him knocking her into several other couples, while he went sliding up onto the stage, knocking the singer into the keyboard player.

"Sorry," she mumbled, twisting around, mortified. She was grateful to feel someone else grab her other hand.

"You don't mind if I steal your lovely girlfriend away for a few minutes do you?" Ava asked as Jared rolled back down to the floor, her tone and expression completely innocent.

"Huh?" he questioned, straightening up and seemingly disoriented. "Uh ... no. I'll go get another drink."

"Thanks," Holly murmured to her sister as she stumbled toward their empty table, still trying to get her balance back.

"You seemed like you could use rescuing. What's with him anyway?"

"Oh, the usual. Too much to drink, and now he's making an ass out of himself. Don't worry. At the rate he's going, he'll be passed out before dinner is served. I'll just prop him up on a chair in the lobby, and you won't even know he's here. We can drape coats over him or something."

Ava laughed. "Sounds like a plan. Hey, we could put out a tip basket and give the coat room some competition."

Holly joined in the laughter as they took a seat at the bridal table. She was grateful for a chance to give her feet a rest. Between walking around all day in high-heels and the nightmarish dance escapade with Jared, sitting felt like heaven. She peeked over to the table across the room. *He* was back.

"Hey, Ava," she started, "do you know—"

"Oh, Hol," her sister interrupted. "Have you ever met Cynthia?"

A beautiful older woman with perfectly styled platinum hair, wearing a gorgeous blue silk gown, approached their table.

"From the gallery?" Holly asked, her aching feet protesting as she rose.

Cynthia nodded. "You must be one of Ava's sisters. She's talked so much about you both, I feel like I already know you. Now let me guess—gorgeous blonde hair, stunning blue eyes. You must be Holly?"

"Yes, that's right. And thank you."

"Well, it's a pleasure to finally meet."

"And you as well," she replied, taking the hand Cynthia held out to her.

Ava stood up, too. "One of these days I need to make a trip back to Wolfenson to visit. I haven't been there in so long. I really miss it."

"It hasn't been the same without you," Cynthia told her, letting some sadness through in her voice. "From what I hear, you're doing quite well for yourself out in California. It sounds like the Silver Leaf Gallery is the talk of the town."

"I don't know about that, but I do love working there. I still can't thank you enough for helping me get my job. It's been a dream come true."

Holly could tell by the woman's warm smile how much she admired her sister. "You wouldn't have gotten the job if you didn't deserve it." Cynthia turned to Holly. "Are you in the art field as well?"

"Me?" She tried to hold back her laughter. "No. I can barely draw a stick figure. Ava was blessed with all the talent in our family."

"Oh, now, my sister is being modest. Holly teaches math to fifth graders. If you ask me, that takes much more talent than anything I do."

"Indeed! Well, I'll let you two get back to the rest of your guests. It was lovely to meet you, Holly, and Ava, I hope we can chat more before you head back." She kissed each of the sisters on both of their cheeks, in a very high-fashioned style, before walking off toward another group of guests.

"I can see why you like her," Holly said. She looked back over to where the mystery man was sitting, now deep in conversation with the man next to him.

"Ah, so this is where my beautiful bride is hiding," Max said, leaning in to give Ava a kiss. "Jared seems like he's having fun, Hol, eh?"

Glancing over to the dance floor, she braced herself for whatever he was up to now. She shook her head as she watched. He was on the ground, in the center, doing some sort of pseudo-breakdancing move, while a circle of women surrounded him, clapping their hands. In all honesty, it looked more like he was squirming around on his back trying to peek up their skirts.

"Yeah." Holly couldn't keep the sarcasm from her voice, rolling her eyes in disgust as she watched the man she hoped to marry one day make a spectacle of himself.

"Are you okay?" Ava asked gently.

"I'm fine," she answered, curling her lips into a sorry excuse for a smile.

"Well if you're sure ..." Ava peered over to a group of people Holly didn't recognize. "Those are some of the artists we've hosted over the years at the gallery."

"Go. You need to mingle, " Holly said, squeezing her hands. "I'm good—I promise."

"Okay," Ava said, giving both Max and Holly pecks on the cheek, before sauntering off.

"Yep, I'm just fine," she said again. Holly stood there with Max as they watched Ava kiss the artists the same way Cynthia had kissed them moments before.

"She's become quite the business woman." A tender expression crossed Max's face as he watched his wife.

"It's nice to see her so excited about her career," Holly agreed.

"It's been a rough road. First she had the difficult pregnancy and then separation anxiety leaving Jenna to go back to work. It was easier when I was helping out with childcare, but I've been flying a lot more for work these days, so I'm not around as much. She loves her job, but it kills her to leave Jenna with the nanny. She puts up a good front though, doesn't she?" Max seemed worried as he watched Ava mingle with their guests. "I should probably go join her."

Studying her brother-in-law, Holly pondered the information he'd shared. She had no idea Ava was struggling to balance work and parenting. She'd never mentioned it to her before. But then she supposed if Ava wanted her to know, she'd have said something. Sighing, she glanced over to the other table again. *He* was still there.

"Wait. Before you go, do you know that guy sitting over there? He looks familiar to me."

"That's my cousin, Ben," he told her.

"Ben … Oakes?" she asked. *His cousin?*

"Yeah," Max said. "You know him?"

Holly nodded, still watching him from across the room. "We went to high school together."

4

"Excuse me," Holly said hesitantly, standing to the side of where he sat deep in conversation with the person sitting next to him. She hated to be rude, but she knew if she didn't speak up right then, she'd completely lose her nerve and walk away. "Ben?"

He glanced over his shoulder, and she saw his lips turn up in a smile. "Ah, so it is you! Holly Haines. I thought it was ... I mean, of course, it had to be. Ava's your sister. You just look so different. Sit, please." Standing, he pulled out the empty chair beside his own.

"Ben," said the man he'd been talking with, "it was great to see you. Glad we could catch up." They shook hands before he walked off.

"I'm so sorry," she said. "I didn't mean to interrupt."

"No, not at all." He sat back down next to her. "That was an uncle I hadn't seen in years. To be honest, I barely even remembered his name, and he was boring me to tears going on and on about a trip to Pittsburgh he took to sell dental products. Or maybe it was Cleveland. He lost my attention about ten minutes ago." He chuckled. "So, Holly Haines. Wow. Max is my cousin. I didn't crash the party here, in case you were wondering."

"No," she laughed. "I figured you were invited. Does that make us related now?"

Peering up at the ceiling as if deep in thought, he smiled. "Hmm ... I don't think so," he said. "So how have you been? I don't think I've seen you since high school. I barely recognized you. You've grown up quite a bit. I mean ... that didn't come out right. You look ... great." He shook his head and turned red.

Holly put her hands up to her face to try to hide her own blushing cheeks. "Thanks, I think, and you look about the same ... different haircut. And you used to wear glasses, right?"

"Yup. I finally made the switch to contacts and got rid of those awful metal frames. The hair probably looks different because I traded in that feathered back rock star wanna-be do for something a little more current."

Holly laughed. She had to admit he looked good. *Really good.* Although she always thought he was one of the cutest guys in her school.

He picked up his drink, and she couldn't help but notice he wasn't wearing a ring. No date and no ring. Interesting. *Stop it, Holly. You're here with your boyfriend. Your live-in boyfriend, remember?*

She watched as Jared staggered across the floor, tripping over his own feet. The good news was he narrowly missed crashing into the three-tiered wedding cake. The bad news was that he stumbled into an elderly woman instead. She wound up with his drink down the front of her dress ... and by the way she was screaming at him, she was *not* happy. Holly shut her eyes as if trying to erase the scene from her memory.

"So, do you still live in Forest Hills?" Ben asked, bringing her attention back to the conversation.

"Hmm? Oh yes, I do," she replied. "I'm a teacher at West Place Elementary."

"No kidding! That's where I went to school."

"Did you? I was at East Place. We've got a few old geezers left at West. I'll bet you know some of them. What about you? Are you still in town?" She was more curious to learn about his present status. They could always reminisce about old teachers later.

"Yup, I can't seem to get away. I manage the plastics plant in the industrial park."

"You don't say. My dad worked there for years."

"I know," he said with a smile. "He's the one who hired me as his replacement."

Holly cocked her head and grinned. "Small world. Well, I have to warn you, he left because of the stress. His blood pressure was through the roof. He's got a nice cushy desk job now."

Ben nodded. "I'll keep that in mind."

"It's funny I haven't run into you all this time. You know, I still have that picture of us from the dance during our sophomore year."

"Get out!" Laughing, she admitted, "So do I. Our outfits were something else, weren't they?"

"I don't know who had more ruffles, you or me." He cringed in shame before breaking out in a belly laugh with her.

"They wouldn't have been so bad if they weren't pastel yellow. We looked like two sticks of butter ... ruffled butter. Maybe we should destroy the evidence ASAP. You don't suppose there are more copies floating around, do you?"

"I don't know," he said, "but I'm all for getting rid of them. I've got a shredder all ready to be fired up for those suckers."

What's it been—ten years since that dance?"

"Just about, yes."

Taking a sip of her drink, Holly tried to think of something else to say. They'd reached the point of awkward silence after discussing high school, bad fashion, and what they currently did for a living. She'd purposely left out Jared. He wasn't really worth talking about, especially after his behavior tonight. Scanning the room, she searched for him. He seemed to be missing. Maybe he'd already passed out in the lobby. Hopefully someone made sure he was on a chair or couch and not sprawled out across the floor.

Ben hadn't brought up a significant other either. So what now? The weather? She watched the bubbles in her champagne while listening to the band.

"This kind of reminds me of that dance," Ben said, breaking the silence between them. "... minus the bride and groom part, of course."

She looked around at the crowd on the dance floor. "It kind of does," she agreed. "With a lot less ruffles, thank goodness."

The sophomore dance, the Soph Hop, was *the* big social event in tenth grade. Holly had been feeling depressed because no one had asked her to go. Specifically, Ben hadn't asked her to go. After much prodding from Ava, she'd decided to invite him instead. It had taken every last ounce of courage to work up the nerve, but she finally did it, and had been thrilled when he said yes.

The night of the dance had been a dream come true for her. From start to finish it was like a fairytale. Then, at the stroke of midnight, her prince dropped her back home with a gentle kiss to her lips. She'd thought her life couldn't possibly get any better than it was at that moment. Sadly, the next day he barely spoke to her, completely breaking her heart.

"I had a really good time with you that night. I … I wanted to ask you out after, but I was so painfully shy back then. I didn't actually know how to act around girls. I hope you didn't think it was because I didn't like you or anything."

She looked up at him in shock. All this time—she wished she had known. "You were my first kiss," she said, smiling bashfully.

Gazing at her, he grinned. "You were my first kiss, too."

She sat for a second, staring into his eyes. She'd always thought he had the most amazing eyes. *He still did.* "I'm glad you told me, and for the record, I would have gone out with you."

"Damn," he said, shaking his head.

"Talking about that dance sure does bring back a lot of memories. Hey, remember that girl who jumped on stage and started doing some weird dirty dancing impersonation? The football team was pretty bummed that the chaperones pulled her outside before her top came off. What was her name? Mindy?"

"Michelle," he said.

"That's right, Michelle. Michelle Floyd. Now I remember. She had quite a reputation through high school, didn't she? I wonder what ever happened to her. Do you know?"

"Yeah," he said. "She's my girlfriend."

Holly opened her mouth to say something, but was interrupted by the lead singer of the band. *"If everyone could please take their seats, dinner is about to be served."*

"I'm— I didn't mean—" she managed to stammer before whirling out of her seat and running off. Seems Jared wasn't the only one to make an ass out of himself that evening.

5

"What is the matter with you?" Tessa asked, a snippy tone in her voice. "You've barely said two words since we started eating. I have to say, you haven't been a very fun date. Are you still upset about Jared?"

"What?" Holly answered, too distracted to pay much attention to what her sister was saying. "No."

As predicted, Jared never made it to dinner, although he wasn't propped up on a chair somewhere in the lobby as originally planned. Instead, Max and Ava decided it was time to let him sleep it off in the honeymoon suite for a bit. He couldn't get into any trouble in there … at least Holly hoped not.

"I'm okay. Embarrassed, but okay." She felt bad her lousy mood was affecting Tessa.

She watched as Ava and Max glided across the dance floor. Did they ever have problems, or was their relationship always as perfect as it seemed to be?

"Oh, don't worry about Jared." Tessa wrapped her arm around Holly's shoulder. "We're all used to him. It's part of his charm," she said with a reassuring squeeze.

Holly furrowed her brow. Was she joking? It wasn't *charming* at all. Anyway, her boyfriend had little to do with her state of embarrassment at the moment. Truth be told, as much as she hated his behavior, she was sadly used to it. That didn't mean it was okay or *charming*, it just meant she wasn't surprised by it anymore. She'd deal with him later. Right now she had other things on her mind.

"See that guy over there?" Holly asked, motioning to Ben's table.

"The one who keeps staring at you? He's a hottie."

"Don't look at him! Pretend you're eating. I know him from high school. We went to this dance together when I was in tenth grade, the Soph Hop. You probably don't remember—you were just a little kid."

"Oh yeah," Tessa said, trying to adjust her body so she wasn't directly facing him. "I do remember! You wore that crazy yellow dress with all the ruffles. I thought you were Lil Bo Peep's long lost sister or something. Not a flattering choice. He looks different without the glasses and pimples." She glanced over at him quickly. "I know I'm not supposed to be looking, but um, he's headed this way."

"What?" Holly squealed, sinking into her seat. "Oh crap." She ducked down, her head under the table, pretending she'd dropped her napkin.

"Holly?" Ben asked. "Did you lose something?"

"Huh?" She bumped her head as she came up. "*Shit.*"

"Are you okay?"

"Yes," she muttered, trying to shake off both the physical pain and lingering humiliation from their earlier conversation. "Have you met my sister, Tessa?"

"Ah," her sister said, "so this is the Soph Hop date. *Ow!*" She yelped in response to Holly's kick under the table. "Nice to meet you," she said, grinning through gritted teeth. "*Again.*"

"Nice to see you again, too," he said, a smile playing at the corner of his lips as he turned his attention back to Holly. "Would you like to dance?"

"Oh. I don't know if I ..."

"Just go!" Tessa ordered, shoving Holly's chair out with her foot, practically dumping her out of her seat in the process.

"Um, sure, thanks," she said, glaring at her sister. Following him to the front of the room, she hoped the song the band chose to play wasn't a long one.

Holly reached one hand up to his shoulder, allowing him to take her other in his. They stayed an awkward distance apart as they moved to the music. Even in heels, she was still considerably shorter than he was. She'd always been the shortest of the three sisters. Somewhere in the gene pool, she'd lost out in the height department. If she looked straight ahead, she'd be staring at his neck, so she decided to look off to the side instead.

"I'm sorry—" they both began at the same time.

"No ... you go," they both continued. Their light chuckles seemed to be exactly what she needed to relax a little. Turning her head, she gazed up at him.

"Please," Ben told her, "go ahead."

"I just ..." Holly began, closing her eyes for a moment. "I feel terrible about what I said, about Michelle. That was sixteen-year-old gossipy teenage me talking, not twenty-five-year-old mature adult me. To be honest, I didn't know her at all in school, and it was a long time ago—I'm sure she's a great girl. Besides, I'm not exactly one to pass judgment. My boyfriend is upstairs sleeping off his drinking binge. He was the guy on the dance floor who slid into the band earlier? Yeah. I'm going to pull my very large foot out of my mouth now."

"That's your boyfriend?" He laughed, and then cleared his throat. "Sorry. No, I was going to apologize, too. I shouldn't have blurted it out like that. I know I caught you off-guard. Like you said, it was a long time ago. When I first met her, I didn't even realize it was the same person until we got to talking."

"So you two haven't been together since high school?" Holly asked. She didn't remember Michelle having a steady boyfriend back then. She preferred to ... move around.

"No. We didn't even know each other in high school. Not really. I mean I knew who she was, but we never dated or anything. We actually only met this past summer."

"You don't say." Holly glanced around, more interested in Michelle's current whereabouts and less interested in the story of how they met. From what she could tell, Ben had come to the wedding alone. "So, is Michelle here?"

"She's on a business trip. She's the Director of Marketing for her company. They're based out of Manhattan."

"Does she travel a lot?"

"Not too often. These days, most of her work can be done remotely, but every now and again they want to see a human. The timing isn't always the best."

Holly couldn't tell if he sounded sad or annoyed, but she could tell Michelle's schedule did not make him happy.

The music ended, but Ben still held on to Holly, staring down at her. She thought she saw something in his eyes, a spark maybe. Perhaps she was imagining things.

She caught sight of her family standing in front of the bridal table. "I, um, I should be getting back.

Looks like Ava's getting ready to throw the bouquet. She promised to aim it at me. It was great seeing you again. Thanks for the dance."

"Same here," he said, his hand lingering at her waist a few seconds longer before slowly letting her go. He began to head toward his table, but turned back around. "Hey, good luck," he added.

"Good luck?"

"Yes," he said, motioning to the crowd of women starting to surround the bride. "With the bouquet catching, I mean."

She smiled. "Thanks."

6

"Honestly, Jared! At my own sister's wedding!" Holly paced their bedroom, fuming, pausing to slam dresser drawers, as she changed out of her gown and into a sweatshirt and yoga pants.

"Could you tone it down a little, Hol? My head is pounding." He lay curled on the bed, looking like hell.

"I'll bet," she said, struggling to pull the sweatshirt over her head. Her hair was still in its fancy up-do from the wedding. "You're lucky Jenna's asleep in the next room, otherwise I'd really be making some noise." As far as she was concerned, he'd earned every ounce of misery he was feeling now. She placed the silk gown into the garment bag, hanging it in her closet, and began the painstaking process of removing the fifty or so bobby pins that had held her hair perfectly in place all evening.

"You're doing a pretty good job already," he mumbled, before jumping up and racing to the bathroom.

As the reception started to wind down, Max and Holly went up to the honeymoon suite to check on Jared. Kick him out was more like it, since Max kind of wanted to use it for Ava and himself at that point. They'd expected to find Jared fast asleep. Instead, they found him hunched over the toilet getting sick. Max helped him get cleaned up while Holly went back downstairs to get Jenna and say good-bye. She was looking forward to spending quality time with her niece while Ava and Max took a short honeymoon before returning to California.

He stumbled back over to the bed, appearing a bit green, but unapologetic. "It was a party, and they had an open bar. They wanted people to drink."

"They wanted people to have a *few* drinks each," she said, "not drink enough to pass out before the food was served."

"So I drank a little too much, what's the big deal?"

Why didn't he care? Did he enjoy feeling this way? She didn't understand.

"You always drink too much. This happens every time we go out, Jared. Every. Time. You do realize that, don't you?" Even after all of the hairpins were out, her hair stayed in perfect formation on top of her head. She attempted to run her brush through it to separate the strands. After the third attempt, her long blonde hair fell over her shoulders. A good shampoo would remove whatever hairspray remained.

Picking up the bouquet she'd caught at Ava's wedding, she twirled it between her fingers. "I don't know why I thought tonight would be any different. I guess I'm the idiot who thought *maybe* this time you'd be a little more mature since it was my sister's wedding—a wedding that might even have some sort of effect on you—*maybe* get you thinking. Apparently, the only thing you were thinking about was how much fun you could have."

"Isn't that what you're supposed to do at weddings? Have a good time? I'm sorry. Next time, I'll just sit at the table quietly with my hands folded neatly across my lap and not move. Oh, I know ... I'll even bring something to read. *The Wall Street Journal*, perhaps? Help me out here, 'cause it seems like you're talking about more than me getting drunk."

Holly *was* talking about more than his drinking, but now wasn't the time to get into it ... at least not *all* of it ... not the part about how she was getting tired of always being the bridesmaid and never the bride. She really thought—hoped—he would want their relationship to experience the same level of passion and commitment she craved—especially after witnessing the deep love Ava and Max had for each other. Didn't he want that? Maybe, but he was obviously too drunk to notice. Now wasn't the time to get into it. She had plenty of other things from the night to be pissed about.

"You're right. It wasn't just the drinking. It was the being loud, knocking into stuff, the ridiculous dancing—the *flirting*. It was embarrassing, for me and for you. You nearly took out the entire band and the wedding cake. Do you know how much that cake cost? Not to mention the fact that you spilled one of your drinks all over Max's eighty-year-old aunt. Do you even remember that? The poor lady nearly broke a hip trying to get out of your way before you almost knocked her over. I told her to send us her dry-cleaning bill."

He laughed. "Oh yeah. That old biddy was cursing at me. I do remember, now that you mention it. She was a spunky one. Nothing funnier than hearing an old hag yell *dickhead*."

"It's not funny, Jared! That woman is part of my sister's family. You should be ashamed of yourself."

He rolled his eyes. "Oh, stop being so dramatic. Just because you don't know how to have a good time, doesn't mean the rest of us shouldn't enjoy ourselves." He laid back on the bed, putting his hands behind his head.

"Really, Jared? *Really?* Was rolling around the floor like a pig, trying to peek up girls' skirts, what you call having a good time? Yeah, I saw you doing that, and so did everyone else. That was a real shining moment for me. *Hey, everyone, check out my boyfriend! Isn't he dreamy? Don't you wish he was yours? Sorry, ladies, he's all mine! But if you want to line up, you can give him a cheap thrill.* Woohoo! Aren't I the lucky one?"

She placed the bouquet back down on her dresser. So she caught it, big deal. She should have let Tessa catch it. Why did her sisters both insist Ava throw it to her? It wasn't like she'd be getting married soon anyway.

"When are you going to grow up? You're not in college anymore. And even in college, this behavior would be unacceptable."

"Geez, Holly, lighten up! You're acting like my mother, not my girlfriend."

"Well maybe if you acted like an adult, I'd treat you like one. Two-hundred and fifty guests, and you were the only one who passed out before dinner."

"Don't forget, Jenna. She passed out before dinner, too," he said, chuckling.

"She's a toddler, and I'm not laughing."

"Whatever. I can't talk to you when you're like this. I have a headache, the room is spinning, and I just want to rest. Why don't you come give me some loving and help your old man fall asleep?" He reached out to try to pull her toward the bed.

Disgusted, she stepped aside. "You're right, I'm not your mommy. I've already got more than enough kids in my classroom at school. Right now, I'm looking for a man. It's up to you to decide if you can be one or not."

She grabbed her pillow and stormed out the door. She'd be more than happy to snuggle with Jenna in the guest room tonight.

7

"**A**unt Holly, Aunt Holly, wake up!"

"Mmmm ..." Holly opened her eyes to see Jenna peering down at her. Her chubby little finger still poking her cheek despite the fact she was now awake.

"Hi, sweetie."

The early morning sun shone through the cracks in the blinds hanging in the guest room. She'd have to try to adjust those so they didn't let in as much light tomorrow morning. She'd forgotten little kids woke up so early. She only had a few days off before she had to be back at school, and she wanted to be able to sleep in—at least a little bit. It was one of the few luxuries she rarely had a chance to enjoy. "Do you want to watch a little TV? Aunt Holly just wants to sleep for a few more minutes." She reached for the remote, but Jenna pulled it out of her hands before she could click the power button.

"No! No TV. You have to get up. We have a surprise!"

"Surprise? We?" Rubbing her eyes, she tried to shake off her fatigue and noticed her niece had a huge grin across her face. "What's going on? What's that smell?"

Jenna was hopping up and down. "Come on, Aunt Holly, come on!"

"Okay, okay." She pushed the covers to the side. How could she resist the adorable wide-eyed girl standing next to her? She could always sleep later.

Her niece took her hand, pulling her out of the guest room and into the kitchen of the apartment she shared with Jared. She couldn't help but stop and smile. The kitchen table, a plain folding table they'd picked up at a yard sale, was covered with one of her fancy tablecloths—the ones she used whenever they had company. On top sat a bud vase with a single red rose. Propped up against that was an envelope with Holly's name written across it. In front of the vase and card was a plate of food: eggs, pancakes, and her favorite—a chocolate chip muffin—along with a cup of coffee.

"What's all this?" she asked, her tone suspicious.

Jared, who was leaning against the kitchen counter, grinned. Either his hangover was gone, or he had learned over the years how to successfully hide it. Holly knew the latter was most likely the case.

"This," he said, pulling the chair out for her, "is my way of saying I was a big jerk last night."

"Ooh, he said a bad word," Jenna tattled.

Holly stifled a giggle. She was still mad at Jared, but he *was* making an effort to apologize. He earned points for that. She could feel her anger slipping away, although she wasn't quite ready to forgive him yet. She sat down and picked up her fork.

"I helped cook," Jenna announced, bouncing up and down beside her, obviously thrilled at having been a part of the surprise.

"Oh did you now? Did you make the eggs?"

"Uh, huh. I helped stir them, and I told Uncle Jared to make the pancakes like hearts."

She stared at the lopsided ovals on her plate. "These are hearts?" she teased, glancing at Jared.

He shrugged and nodded, a shy smile crossing his face.

"Mommy makes me heart pancakes all the time. Except hers look like hearts. I miss Mommy ... and Daddy. Are they coming to get me soon?"

"Oh, honey." Holly picked her up and balanced her on her lap, "Mommy and Daddy are on their honeymoon. Do you know what that is?"

"Their wedding vacation?"

"Yes," she grinned, trying not to giggle. She loved Jenna's innocence. She missed so much of her niece's life with her sister living clear across the country. Holly was so happy to have this time to spend with her and dreamed of the day she'd be able to snuggle a little one of her own on her lap like this every day. "Yes, their wedding vacation. They'll be gone for a few days, but we're going to have lots of fun. Aunt Tessa's going to stop by later to take you out, and tomorrow you're going to Grandma and Grandpa's house for a few days. Mommy and Daddy will be back before you know it. I'll bet they'll call you later."

She gave her aunt a hug before she jumped off her lap. "Can I watch TV now?"

"Sure," Holly said, glad her moment of *missing Mommy and Daddy sadness* seemed to be over.

"I'll go get her set up," Jared offered. "You eat before your food gets cold."

She took a bite of her eggs and opened her envelope. He must have gone out to the twenty-four hour market at the crack of dawn to put all of this together. She pulled out the card. It was one of those mushy ones with a couple on the cover that said, "I'm sorry" in fancy script. Inside were more passages asking for forgiveness and professing the writer's love, including a handwritten note stating how lucky he was to have her in his life. In the three years they'd been dating, he'd never bought her a card for an occasion other than her birthday or Valentine's Day. Even then, it always had a joke or sarcastic remark attached to it—usually referring to her as the old ball and chain, or something like that. Was this the same Jared? She took another bite of the eggs.

"How's the food?" he asked, coming back into the kitchen.

"It's good, thanks," she replied, laying the card beside her plate. She gazed up at him with a hint of an apprehensive glint in her eyes.

He pulled out the chair next to her and sat down. "I really am sorry, you know. Humiliated, to tell you the truth. I thought a lot about what you said last night after you left the room, and you were right. My behavior was awful. It's not going to happen again, I can promise you that. I plan on calling your parents later to apologize."

Holly raised her eyebrows. "Okay," she said slowly and pinched herself under the table. Was she still asleep? This had to be a weird dream, right? She wasn't *actually* sitting next to Jared—her Jared— listening to him apologize. He never apologized, not like this. *Call her parents?* The next thing she knew he'd propose to her. She started choking on her eggs.

"Hol? Are you okay?" He jumped up and ran behind her.

She brought her hands up to her throat, and panic set in as she realized she couldn't draw in a breath. Jared wrapped his arms around her torso, and with a hard thrust, the offending piece of egg flew out of her mouth and across the table. She gasped for air.

No, she was most definitely not dreaming. "Thank you," she whispered. "Thank you."

He buried his head in her hair. "I'm so sorry, baby, I really am. I realized last night after you went to the guest room how miserable I'd be without you. We were meant to be together, you know. Forever. And I'll do whatever it takes to make that happen, to prove to you I'm the man that's meant to be in your life. I just want you to be happy, for us to be happy. I love you, Hol. I love you so much."

She wiped away the tears that were streaming down her face, and turned around to hug him. "I love you, too, babe. Always."

Holly sat in the staff meeting watching the clock. School officially ended at three. She'd planned on staying until three-thirty to get ahead on lesson plans—then she'd wanted to hit the grocery store on her way home. She and Jared were completely out of food. Her dinner last night consisted of frozen waffles and peanut butter. It was reminiscent of her college days.

Jared had eaten at the hospital cafeteria. He was on the maintenance crew at Crestmont Memorial and had worked the evening shift last night. He liked to tell people he was involved in some of the construction projects at the hospital, but in reality he spent most of his eight hours changing light bulbs in the ceilings and batteries in the IV pumps. Holly reminded herself regularly everyone had to start somewhere.

Her phone buzzed. She tried to muffle the sound with her hands, so as not to disrupt the meeting, while discreetly reading the message.

Want to grab a drink tonight?

Just as Holly was about to leave earlier, Dan Harper, the newly hired principal of her school, popped his head into her classroom to say he wanted to hold an impromptu staff meeting at four o'clock with the math teachers. "*Certainly,*" she'd responded with a fake smile. According to her contract, she was supposed to stay at school until four-thirty, so she couldn't exactly say she'd planned on leaving an hour early.

Dan Harper insisted his staff call him by his first name when out of earshot of the students. Around them, he was still to be Mr. Harper, of course. However, despite his request, most of the senior staff still called him Mr. Harper, whether there were students present or not. The principal before him, Mrs. Sinclair, had been there forty years and had *always* been referred to as Mrs. Sinclair. Nobody would dare call her Elizabeth, even behind her back. Holly supposed old habits were hard to break. She had no problem calling him Dan.

She peeked at the clock: four-fifteen. She hid her phone behind her stack of books while she typed, feeling like she was back in high school.

Sorry, Tess. Long day. I'm beat. Rain check?

There were two other math teachers besides herself at West Place Elementary. Gus Shaw, a pudgy, balding man who occasionally filled in for the gym teacher, and Elaine Fairview, a silver-haired, wrinkly woman who looked like she was old enough to have taught Holly's parents.

Elaine mainly taught the sixth-graders and was constantly complaining about either her students or the curriculum, stating the former were too unruly and the latter was too difficult. Holly found it funny she chose education as her profession since she appeared to have such a low tolerance for both children and teaching. Elaine also insisted *everyone*, including Dan Harper, call her Mrs. Fairview. Oddly enough, however, she wasn't one of the ones who called him Mr. Harper. Holly wondered if *Mrs. Fairview* knew everyone called her Elaine behind her back.

Gus was the math coordinator for the lower grade teachers. He didn't actually teach math to any students. Instead, he taught the curriculum to the first through fourth grade teachers, who then taught it to their own students. It seemed like a nice, cushy job that had an awful lot of downtime. Holly was just glad she didn't have to deal with him on a regular basis. On the weird meter, Gus ranked above average.

Her phone buzzed again.

What about tomorrow? I haven't talked to you since the wedding.

At four-thirty, Dan Harper continued to drone on about motivating students to engage in more critical thinking.

Cereal, and milk, and ... he's got nice teeth, Holly thought while wondering if Jared would be home in time for dinner ... *oh right, and I need eggs.*

She'd forgotten to ask Jared what time his shift was over when she spoke with him earlier that day. Poor guy had arrived home at six in the morning and then had to be back to work at noon. The old Jared would have told his boss to go to hell, but the new Jared said it was no problem. He'd been trying to stay on his boss' good side lately. In fact, he'd been trying to stay on her good side, too. So far he was doing a decent job.

They'd barely seen each other today, although they did manage to make love this morning before she had to leave for work. He was even doing a better job in that department, however, she'd never had any complaints where that was concerned. Even so, he seemed different in bed—more attentive, romantic. She couldn't put her finger on it exactly ... she just knew it was better. Thinking about it, she smiled.

"I see that grin, Holly," Dan stated. "Does that mean I can count you in?"

She looked up at him. *Crap. What had he asked? Did it matter? He was her boss, she had to agree.*

"Yup, sure thing," she answered with a corny thumbs up.

"Great, we'll meet back here tomorrow after school to get started. I think the kids are really going to enjoy this."

Holly nodded. *Awesome, another meeting to talk about something I apparently signed up for.* This new principal was too much. She collected her things and headed out the door, texting as she walked toward her car:

Sure, Tessa, I'll call you after my staff meeting tomorrow afternoon.

9

"So things are good with Jared?" Ava asked.

Holly tried to balance the phone between her ear and shoulder as she unloaded the groceries.

It was hard to believe two weeks had passed already since the wedding. It felt like yesterday, although Holly missed her sister terribly. October was flying by.

After their week-long honeymoon, they only stayed in town one additional night before heading back to California with Jenna. Between Ava's hectic schedule at the gallery and the time difference from living on different coasts, their communications seemed to be limited to quick texts lately. Yes, she was glad to have

Tessa around, but it wasn't the same. Ava had always been Holly's number one confidant.

"You wouldn't believe it," Holly said, finally deciding to set the phone on the counter, switching over to speaker mode. She stacked up the packages of meat with one hand while pulling the freezer door open with the other. "Ever since your wedding, he's a changed man, and it's just been getting better."

"Maybe he had an epiphany," Ava laughed. "We were in church you know."

"Actually, I think it was more of him getting a taste of my crazy side when we got home. He's probably terrified to do anything to upset me now." She chuckled as she folded up the empty paper bags from the grocery store. "Don't worry, I made sure Jenna was fast asleep before I completely let him have it. I have to admit, my speech was impressive—and apparently effective."

Pulling a spoon out of the kitchen drawer, she dug right into the tub of ice cream sitting on the counter. It was six o'clock. She'd hoped to get home earlier, but the staff meeting had dragged on forever. Now that her kitchen was fully stocked again, she should probably think about having something for dinner other than Rocky Road.

"Or maybe that bouquet is actually working," Ava said. "You never know, Hol. Three years is a long time to be dating someone."

Three years *was* a long time.

"Maybe," she responded, smiling as she took another spoonful.

She didn't want to say anything more to jinx it. Over the past two weeks, there had been hints. A comment here, a comment there … then yesterday Jared mentioned he asked his boss for a raise. Said it was so he could start saving up for something *special*. His boss told him he would think about it, but Jared had sounded so hopeful. She was trying to be supportive, not asking any questions. She didn't want to ruin the surprise—or her boyfriend's good mood. Holding out her left hand, she tried to imagine a how it would look with a sparkling engagement ring wrapped around her finger.

"How's work going?" Ava asked, not waiting to see if Holly had anything more to say on the subject.

Her sister always knew the perfect moment to stop pushing and move on to something else. Holly loved that about her.

"It's good," she answered. "I have a really great group of kids. Some of the parents are a little much, but you know—there's always one or two every year. Promise me you won't be one of *those* parents."

"What? You mean like Mom?"

"Exactly. I do like our new principal, though. I was a little nervous about him at first since he's young and inexperienced, but I'm young and inexperienced, too. For the most part, he seems like he knows what he's doing. Except for his staff meetings. They drag on forever, and he likes to have a lot of them. Like today's. It was over an hour. I couldn't help but zone out, during which time I think I volunteered for a committee or something. Let's just hope for the sake of the kids it's not the annual bake sale. *That* would be a disaster. Otherwise he's good, and he's nice to look at.

"Is he now?" Ava asked.

"Oh, stop. Not like that. I have Jared. Besides, you get to look at pretty artwork all day at your job," Holly said. "Who says I can't have something nice to look at where I work as well?"

"Um, I work in an *art gallery?*"

"A minor detail," she teased. "But seriously, the kids seem to like him. I think he's going to work out okay. Much better than that cranky old Mrs. Sinclair. Thank God she finally decided to retire. I was about to start putting my resume out for a position at another school."

"Well, good. I'm glad it all worked out. But keep your eyes in your head, young lady. You've got a man at home who is moving and shaking, remember?"

"Yeah, yeah," she said, shoving another spoonful of ice cream in her mouth.

"Oh! I forgot to tell you— We're coming out for Thanksgiving next month."

"You are?" Holly swallowed hard to get the words out. "When will you get here?"

"We're flying out to Max's parents' house Tuesday. We'll have turkey and all the fixings with his family on Wednesday and drive to Forest Hills for another Thanksgiving meal with you all on Thursday. We'll stay Friday with Mom and Dad before we fly home Saturday morning. Sorry we can't stay longer. Honestly, it's a miracle Max's company even let him take the holiday off with it being such a hectic season. You know what they say—Thanksgiving is the busiest time for traveling. He got lucky ... he gets to take both Thanksgiving and Christmas. I guess all those years of working holidays is finally paying off. "

"That's awesome! It's like an early birthday present for me," Holly said, smiling. Having an early December birthday was always difficult, as she often got forgotten between the fanfare surrounding Thanksgiving and Christmas.

"I wish we could stay long enough to celebrate with you, but two weeks would be pushing it."

"Well, I'm glad you're able to come at all, even if it's just for a few days. I miss you so much ... and that sweet little girl of yours, too."

"She sure does love her Aunt Holly. Speaking of, I need to go pick her up from school."

"Okay, give her a kiss from me. And one for your hubby, as well."

"Will do, and love to Jared also. I'll talk to you soon. And Holly?"

"Yes?"

"I'm really happy things are going so well. You deserve the best."

"Thanks, Ava. Love you."

"Love you, too."

10

"I thought this was a staff meeting." Holly shifted uncomfortably in the high back leather chair in Dan's office. The balls of her feet barely touched the floor. The seats, left over from Mrs. Sinclair's reign of terror, were enough to intimidate anyone. Holly could see why kids always felt frightened going to the principal's office. "Aren't the others coming?" she asked, wondering what exactly she'd volunteered for. She'd been anxious about it all day.

Dan stood up and walked around to where she was sitting. He leaned back against his desk, his knees almost touching hers, and ran his hands through his hair before flashing his smile.

"I have to tell you," he began. "I was a little nervous when I brought up the idea yesterday. I'm so thrilled you're on board with this. I mean, I knew Elaine—Mrs. Fairview—would never go for it, not that she'd be right for this, anyway." He scrunched up his face and stuck out his tongue. "And well, Gus ... he's a little too odd. I was really hoping for someone exactly like you. I think you're absolutely perfect, to tell you the truth." He curled his lips like a mischievous child and walked back over to his chair.

Had he always had those dimples? "So ... um ... what exactly did you have in mind?" she asked, trying to fish for more information, although she wasn't completely sure she wanted to know.

"Well, I thought we could put together some sort of rap. With numbers," he explained.

"Wrapping paper? I suppose the kids could sell it as part of the holiday store this year. But, I'm not sure we'll be able to make that much. Plus, doesn't the school already do a gift paper fundraiser?" Holly was downright confused. She had to admit, while he might be cute, his idea kind of sucked.

"Not gift wrap," Dan laughed. "Rap—with an R. You know ... gettin' jiggy with number five 'cause two and four are getting down ... or something. Ugh, I'm obviously incompetent when it comes to this. That's why I need you. I heard you have a knack for it."

"Me? No. Oh, well, I did write a poem once for my students a couple of years ago about numbers that

they really liked, but that's about it. Hold on—"
Suddenly she remembered what her boss was talking
about when she started zoning yesterday. "You want
to do a rap with me for the talent show?"

"Yes. You *do* remember agreeing to this yesterday,
don't you? We were talking about getting the kids
more engaged through music, specifically with a math
rap. Wait a minute, you don't have a twin sister who
sat in on the meeting while you were out doing
something else, do you?" He smiled, showing off those
dimples again.

Holly smirked. "No, sorry. I was just a little
distracted when you were talking about it, that's all.
To tell you the truth, I wasn't a hundred percent sure
what I had agreed to."

"Ah, that explains it. So," Dan said, running his
fingers through his hair once more.

His hairstyle reminded her of the types of styles
worn by models—underwear models in particular. Not
that she spent a lot of time staring at underwear
models or anything. It was strictly an observation, as
there happened to be a giant billboard with one on it
next to a building she passed on her way to work every
day. She couldn't help but notice his hair, face, and ...
well, body—clothed at least—shared a remarkable
resemblance.

"Holly?"

Oh crap, she was zoning out again.

"I'm sorry, Dan. It's been a long day. What were you saying?"

He sighed. "I was wondering if I could count you in for the rap at the talent show. You'd have to put up with me for the next couple of months, but I think we could really come up with something fun for the kids. What do you say?"

Closing her eyes for a moment to clear her mind, she took a deep breath before starting, "Yo, yo, let's get on the floor, 'cause I want to tell y'all a story 'bout the number four. You see four alone is pretty great, but add two of them together to get the number eight." She opened her eyes and smiled back at Dan. "Something like that maybe?"

He clapped his hands and jumped up. "I love it! See? I knew you'd be perfect. So the show is just after winter break. I know it's a little early to get started, but I want to make certain we're ready. Should we meet again next week?"

Holly grinned. "Sure."

"Holly, over here!"

She kept her eyes on Tessa's hand, waving at her across the crowded room, until she finally made her way over.

"Wow, it's packed in here," she yelled, "and loud."

"Discount drinks on Hump Day," Tessa shouted back. "College kids are broke, remember? Wednesdays are a big party night."

As she took a step closer to the bar, Holly felt her shoe stick to the ground. *Ugh.* She didn't want to think about what was making the floor so gross. There were definitely some things about college she didn't miss one bit. She ordered two beers and followed Tessa to an empty spot by a ledge in the back corner.

"So what's new?" Tessa asked. "I miss talking to you. You're so busy all the time."

"I could say the same thing about you. How's school going?"

"Fine, I guess. I'm excited for the musical this spring. We're doing *City of Angels.* I just found out I got the position of assistant to the casting director, and I'll be on the production crew this year, *finally.* Apparently you have to wait until your junior year of college before anyone starts to take you seriously. Whatever. We don't start work on it until the winter drama is finished, but at least I have something to look forward to second semester."

"Wow, that's great! I'll definitely come see it. Do you think Mom and Dad will start cutting you some slack about being a theater major now?"

"Are you kidding?" she asked, taking a sip of her beer. "All I hear is '*But why can't you do a dual major like your sister, Ava? She knew just being an art major wouldn't get her far. Look at where she is now thanks to her business degree.'* They don't get it, Hol. I'm not in a typical theater program learning to be an actor. I'm in a theater *production* program. I'm learning about every aspect of the theater. *Including the business side.* But every time I try to explain it to them, all they hear is *blah, theater, blah, blah, theater.* One day, when I'm running *my own* theater, they'll get it, I suppose. I'm so glad I was able to get one of the campus apartments this year. If I had to live at home again, I think I'd go insane." She took a long swig of her drink. "But enough about me. What's up with you?"

"I'm sort of in a production, too," Holly began.

"Really? Tell me more."

"Well, it's not quite as exciting as a college musical. It's an elementary school talent show. I'm going to be doing a rap about math with my principal."

Tessa choked on her beer mid-swallow. "Rap? About math?" she managed to say between coughing and laughing. "Is it open to the public? Because this I have to see … and possibly video tape."

Nodding, Holly giggled. "Just call me M.C. Multiply."

"Let me guess, this was your idea," she said, trying to calm herself down. "Only a math nerd like you would come up with something so crazy."

"Actually, it was my principal." She paused to recall the meeting earlier this afternoon.

"You're smiling. Is he cute?"

"Tessa, I have a boyfriend, remember?"

"So? It's okay to think another guy is cute. Just because you have a boyfriend, doesn't mean you have to be blind to the rest of the male population."

She shook her head and rolled her eyes.

"Anyway, let's get out of here," Tessa suggested, finishing her beer. "The smell is starting to get to me. You want to grab a burger down the street?"

"Sounds good." Grabbing her purse, Holly followed her sister's lead as she tried to navigate through the drunken crowd.

Trying to get out of the bar was no easy feat. Tessa grabbed Holly's hand and pulled her through the unruly mob. Of course, that only lasted about thirty seconds as the partiers quickly separated them. Holly felt like a pinball stuck on play as she bounced around in failed attempts to make her way to the exit sign. Every time she was close to making it out, the force of the crowd pushed her back. Maybe it was more like a Ping-Pong match. She'd surely be covered in bruises ... and beer, which seemed to splash on her with every shove. It gave a whole new meaning to Beer Pong. She finally tumbled out onto the sidewalk like a caged animal being set free.

"Sorry," she said to the back of the black ski jacket she slammed into upon her escape. She hadn't meant to go flying into the guy standing by the telephone pole. She would have much preferred to walk out the door like a civilized human being. Instead, she was forced out as though shot from a cannon like a freakish circus act. She continued to walk down the street with Tessa, not waiting for him to turn around. She was in no mood for some guy's cocky college attitude.

"No prob—" the voice said from behind her. "Holly?"

Startling at the sound of her name, she stopped walking, slowly twisting her head to meet the familiar voice. No, this was most definitely not a cocky college student.

"Ben?" She laughed and walked back over to him. "Wow, we don't see each other for years, and then we bump into each other twice in two weeks. This time literally. Sorry about that ... again. It was a little rough in there."

"I can see that." His eyes gleamed as he smiled down on her. Apparently all was forgiven.

Holly tried to smooth down her hair. She imagined she was a mess after that escapade, and she knew she smelled like a brewery. The stink was beyond overpowering. Hopefully he didn't think she was wasted. It was time to do some damage control.

"Well, I'm not going back in that place … ever, that's for sure. I'm way too old for that scene. I'm not even a big drinker."

"To be honest, I'm a bit surprised you were in there at all," he said, raising his eyebrows. "I didn't take you for a dollar Heinie girl."

"A what?" she asked. She'd been called a lot of things over the course of her life, but she'd never been called a dollar Heinie girl. It didn't sound good. She could feel her cheeks getting hot.

"Dollar Heinies," Tessa repeated, now standing next to Holly, pointing to the sign hanging in the bar window. "You know, Heinekens? They're a dollar every Wednesday here. It's a big deal for us college kids. We usually don't get to drink the good stuff for cheap. That's one of the reasons it's so packed in there."

"Ah," Holly said. "Well, no, I can't say that I am one … even tonight. In fact, I definitely have more Heinie *on* me, than in me." She sniffed her arm and cringed. "Yeah. This will be going to the dry cleaner tomorrow. Tessa, maybe the next time you invite me out on a Wednesday, we can go somewhere where they don't have imported beer on the clearance rack."

Her sister rolled her eyes. "It wasn't *that* bad in there."

"Uh-huh. Ben, you remember my younger sister, Tessa. Apparently *she* is a dollar Heinie girl."

He laughed. "Yes, I do remember. We didn't really get a chance to talk at the wedding."

"Ava's Wedding?" Tessa asked, shaking the hand Ben offered.

"Yes," Holly said. She gave Tessa a strange look as if it would help jar her memory. "He's Max's cousin, and ... he was my Soph Hop date from high school. I introduced the two of you as we were finishing up dinner."

"Right! You're yellow frilly tux guy!"

"Awesome," Ben said. "Is that how I'm forever going to be known in your family?"

"Pretty much," Holly said, grinning.

"Not to worry," Tessa added. "Your choice of attire at Ava's wedding was a big improvement."

"Ah, thank you," he laughed. "I've been redeemed. I swear on all of my most prized possessions to never wear yellow ruffles again ... or any ruffles. That was just a bad fashion trend. Very, very bad—one that will hopefully never come back." He flashed his smile at Holly. She'd forgotten what a great sense of humor he'd always had.

"Agreed. So, um, do you normally hang out around here?" Holly asked, shoving her hands in her pockets to keep them warm. She knew the plant he worked at was not far from campus, but this was kind of a young scene for him—although with that smile and his new and improved haircut, he could probably get any girl in there he wanted.

"No. My car broke down." He pointed to an old blue clunker sitting on the side of the road. "I'm waiting for the tow truck."

"Oh, no. Can I give you a ride somewhere?"

"Thanks, but I've got to stick around for the repair guy," he replied. "Listen, I don't want to hold the two of you up. You seemed like you were headed somewhere. It was great seeing you both again."

Holly couldn't help but notice while he said *both,* he was only looking at her, gazing at her, really.

"Actually, we were going to grab a burger from the place around the corner. Can we bring you something back while you wait?" she asked, her heart fluttering from his stare.

Ben's dark eyes appeared even more intense under the dim light of the setting sun. She'd always loved his eyes. They were almost an exact match to his wavy dark brown hair... yet, she'd never noticed the golden flecks in them until now, or the way they glimmered in just the right amount of light. All these years later, and she was still so attracted to him. *It's okay to think another guy is cute.* Why did Tessa's words suddenly pop into her head? Maybe she really didn't imagine the spark in his eyes at Ava's wedding.

"You know what?" Ben replied. "That would be great. I was just getting off of work, and of course I picked today to skip lunch." He reached into his pants pocket, pulled out his wallet, and handed Holly a twenty. "Thanks."

"My pleasure," she answered, noticing he held her hand a little longer than he probably should have as he placed the money into her palm.

12

"So what's the deal with him?" Tessa asked as they walked back toward Holly's car. They'd brought Ben his burger right as the tow truck pulled up. While they'd offered to stay to make sure everything went okay, he'd insisted they go. They said their goodbyes and decided to head back to Holly's apartment.

"What do you mean?" Holly stopped to fish her keys out of her purse. She knew exactly what Tessa meant. She just wasn't sure how to answer the question. She had Jared, and he was doing all the right things now. And even her sister had said it was okay to think another guy was cute. It's not like she was going to go after him or anything. Besides, even if there were no Jared, Ben was already in a relationship.

"I told you," Holly said, as she and Tessa got into the car, "we've known each other since high school. Besides, he's Max's cousin. I guess that makes us family."

"Not really. I mean, not in a *your DNA could mix and your babies would have three arms* sense."

"How did we jump to making babies with him all of a sudden?"

"It was the way he was staring at you, Hol. I don't know, like he was sizing you up or something. And not in an *I'm your cousin* way. It was more romantic."

"Don't be ridiculous. He has a girlfriend."

"He does? She wasn't at the wedding, was she? If I remember correctly, you and Ben danced—slow danced."

"We did, and she wasn't. She was away on a business trip, but that doesn't mean anything. Jared wasn't there either. Well he was, but he wasn't. You know."

"And why wasn't she here tonight? Helping him when his car broke down? You would have come in a second if Jared's car had broken down."

"Jared doesn't have a car," Holly reminded her. "He takes the bus most of the time."

"I mean if he borrowed yours. Which he does a lot, by the way, when you're not using it. And your car isn't much better than Ben's, no offense."

"Thanks, I think," Holly said, scanning the interior of her car. It was old, yes, but reliable. She'd bought it used when she was in college, and so far, it had been fine.

"My point *is,* if Jared *was* driving your car, and it *had* broken down, you would have figured out a way to get here to help ... and not just because it's your car."

Her sister was right. She would have been there for Jared. Why wasn't Michelle here helping Ben? Hadn't he said she didn't travel much?

"I don't know. He mentioned she's an executive or something. She probably couldn't get out of work, or maybe he didn't call her. Anyway, it's really none of our business."

Holly watched as the driver finished hitching Ben's car up to the tow bar. When they climbed into the cab of the truck, she started her engine and headed in the opposite direction.

"Do you believe in fate?" Tessa asked.

"I don't know, why?"

"I think it's odd, that's all. I mean, what are the chances of running into Ben again after all these years—first at Ava's wedding, then again tonight right as we're leaving the bar. I feel like the universe is trying to tell you something. There was no mistaking the way Ben was looking at you. Trust me."

"It's a small town. We were bound to meet again eventually. I don't think fate, or the universe, had anything to do with it. Besides, if the universe was so interested in reuniting us, why would they give him a girlfriend and me a boyfriend? A boyfriend, who by the way, after three years *finally* wants to have a committed relationship."

Tessa looked over to her sister with a stunned expression. "Are you saying Jared proposed? Why didn't you tell me?" she demanded.

"No, not that," Holly said. "At least not yet, but he's so devoted to our relationship right now. Things between us have never been better. Plus, he's been talking about a big surprise, and you know, my birthday *is* coming up in a couple of months." She felt like a schoolgirl the way she was gushing, but she couldn't help it. Everything she dreamed of was finally falling into place. "He's even hinted at starting a family, and you know how much I want to have children one day. If the universe is trying to say anything, it's that Jared is the one for me."

"So what are you going to do?"

"About what?" Holly asked.

"About Ben? I wasn't imagining what I witnessed back there, Hol. And to be honest, I was getting vibes from you, too."

"I already told you. He has a girlfriend, I have Jared, and you have an overactive imagination. Case closed. Come on. Let's go eat our dinner."

13

"**K**nock, knock. Do you have a minute?"

Holly looked up from her desk to see Gus Shaw standing in the doorway. He must have been filling in for the gym teacher again based on the whistle around his neck and the bright blue oversized mesh tank top, which hung over his red T-shirt and running shorts like a dress. Interesting outfit. *What was he doing here?* She only had one free period before the next group of fifth-graders were due to arrive, and she'd hoped to get a jump on grading homework from the previous class.

"Sure, Gus, what's up?" she asked, regretting the words as she spoke them.

"Well, it's about this talent show," Gus responded, bounding into the room.

"What about it?"

"I know Dan didn't ask me directly, but you may remember I'm actually pretty good with these sorts of things. I guess he didn't know since this is his first year at West Place Elementary."

Holly did her best to hold in her sarcastic remarks. Last year, Gus performed some sort of modern interpretive dance wearing a neon green spandex outfit that covered him from head to toe, including his face. He looked like a monstrous inchworm that escaped from a nuclear science lab. He not only scared the kids, he scared most of the parents and staff as well. She was fairly sure Dan knew about Gus' horrific act.

"I've been giving it some thought," he continued, "and have come up with a few math related ideas for the show. I've also got costumes planned. Believe it or not, I'm pretty good with a sewing machine." He came closer to her desk. She leaned back in her chair as far as she could to avoid his breath as he whispered, "I have a lot of down time, and the sewing room is empty most of the day." He cleared his throat and, thankfully, backed out of Holly's personal space. "Anyway, I thought I could make you look like a giant addition sign, while I could be multiplication." He jumped out like he was doing a jumping jack to make his arms and legs into the shape of an 'X'. "See? There's a ton of fabric left over to work with. I could make them puff out with pillow stuffing, like the Pillsbury Dough Boy." He filled air in his cheeks and walked around with a stiff gait, but looked more like a robot than a lovable squishy icon. "Then we can do a dance together. Or I can play piano and sing, while you do acrobatics. You know, somersaults and whatnot."

"Oh—" she said, not knowing how to even begin to respond.

"That sounds wonderful," Dan interrupted, walking into Holly's classroom, "but I'm afraid Holly has a partner for the talent show. Me. We've already started on something together. It's kind of a surprise, so if you don't mind ..." He took Gus' arm and led him toward the door.

"Okay, okay. Fine," he stammered, "Holly— you can be multiplication!" he yelled in a final plea, as his boss gently pushed him into the hallway.

"We're good, Gus, thanks," Dan said, before closing the door. He collapsed into the chair in front of Holly's desk.

She covered her mouth and burst into a fit of laughter. "Thank you," she said, trying to compose herself so Gus wouldn't hear her. The poor guy might be weird, but he meant well. "You have perfect timing."

"Actually, I really *was* coming in to talk to you about the talent show. I'm not going to be able to meet with you after school as planned."

Holly felt a pang of disappointment.

"Oh, well ..." She wasn't sure how to respond. Disappointed? Indifferent?

"Yeah. Unfortunately, I have to meet with some parents instead." He sneered and rolled his eyes.

"I thought only teachers rolled their eyes at parents. Aren't principals supposed to be more diplomatic and professional?"

Dan leaned in closer. "Only in public. I've got some good stories ... especially from my prior school. I'm sure you've had your share of fun parents as well?"

She nodded and smiled.

"Maybe we can trade tales over lunch today? And talk more about the talent show, you know, so we're not just sitting around making fun of moms and dads who make our jobs harder than they have to be." He winked as he got up.

"Sure." She was a bit stunned at the invitation, and confused about his true intentions. "I have lunch at eleven forty-five."

"Great. Meet you back here with a couple of gourmet sandwiches from our five star cafeteria."

"No!" Holly said with a laugh. "They didn't really say that!" She took the last bite of her sandwich and ran her tongue over her teeth, hoping there were no embarrassing pieces of food stuck there.

"Scouts honor," Dan said, holding up his three fingers in perfect formation. "Apparently they were proud of the fact that their kindergartener had such an advanced vocabulary."

"They do know there are better ways of encouraging language growth other than teaching him curse words, right?"

"That's what I tried to explain."

"What'd they say?"

"What do you think they said?" Dan raised his eyebrows.

"No they didn't!" She started laughing all over again.

"They did!"

"What did you do?"

"You mean after I scraped my chin off the floor? I told them if their child told the teacher to f-off again, he'd be suspended. The next week, I received a notice from the district that the family decided to homeschool."

"Wow, you really have heard it all."

"Pretty much, and I've only been doing this five years." He paused as he propped his elbow on the desk and rested his chin in his hand. Smiling at Holly, he said, "I can't wait to see what the next five brings."

He *was* talking about being a principal, wasn't he?

"I hear kids coming," he continued, sitting back up.

Holly peeked at the clock. Lunch period was way too short, especially when she was in good company. *Good company with cute dimples.*

"I guess our time's up," Dan said, sounding as disappointed as she felt. "I've been going on about my job so much, we never did talk about the talent show. Sorry about that."

"That's okay. Actually, I've been working on our routine a bit. I've got another few lines together ... and some dance steps."

"Dance steps?" he asked, a concerned expression crossing his face.

"Don't worry, it's nothing fancy. I'm not that coordinated. It's more like a stepping back and forth while we rap type thing."

"So we're not talking Gus-style moves," Dan said, chuckling.

"Oh God no!" Holly snorted and cackled at the same time. She brought her hand up to her mouth, embarrassed at the sound that had come out of her. She had to admit, despite her snackle, this was one of the most fun *working* lunches she'd ever had.

"Well, I can't wait to see it. Do you want to meet Thursday after school?"

"Sounds perfect. See you then. And wear your dancing shoes," Holly teased.

14

Holly was in the kitchen cooking breakfast when she heard the apartment door open. The eggs were a tiny bit runny, and the bacon was almost burnt to a crisp—just the way Jared liked it.

"Hol! Where are you? Holly!"

"I'm in the kitchen," she called out. If he'd stop for two seconds to take in the aromas, he'd know exactly where she was. The apartment wasn't that big. She poured a tall glass of orange juice and reached for a plate to start dishing out his food. "Your breakfast is almost ready."

It was ten in the morning, and Jared was getting in from working another overnight at the hospital. He was supposed to work the day shift, but traded with a co-worker so he could have Sunday off. She knew he'd be hungry and tired and wanted to make sure he had a hot meal waiting, as well as plenty of time to catch up on some sleep. They'd be heading out to her parent's house at around three for a visit. A least one Sunday a month Holly's mom liked to have her girls come over for a big family meal.

"Forget breakfast." Jared caught her around the waist and twirled her, nearly knocking her into the pans on the stovetop. He kissed her fully on the lips and spun her around again, before reaching up to the cabinet above the refrigerator to pull down a bottle of wine—the one Holly had been saving to bring to Thanksgiving dinner in a couple of weeks. "We need to celebrate."

"Celebrate?" she asked, looking from the wine to Jared. She couldn't remember the last time she'd seen him so happy. "It's not even noon yet. What's going on?"

"Babe," he started, fishing around one of the kitchen drawers for a corkscrew, "remember how I asked my boss for a raise last month?"

"Yes," she said, her enthusiasm growing with Jared's excitement. She could feel the electricity in the air. "Does this mean he gave it to you?"

He kept searching without answering. When he finally found what he was looking for, he glanced up at her and said, "He did better than that. He gave me a raise *and* a promotion. I'm now the team leader for the second and third floors of the Galloway Wing."

Holly stared at Jared, stunned. She didn't understand all the details, but she knew it was good news. Really good news. He'd been working so hard lately to prove himself. Getting this raise and promotion meant they were one step closer to their goals—not only financially, but on a maturity level, too. It showed Jared was capable of being responsible—that he really did want a future with her.

"Oh, baby, that's amazing! I'm so proud of you. So proud!"

Pulling out the cork, he filled the two mugs Holly had set out for coffee and said, "Here's to the beginning of great things." He clinked his mug to hers before taking a drink. "Great things for both of us," he added, "together."

Yes, she thought, smiling. She was ready for great things for both of them. "Do you want something to eat?" she asked. "I made your favorites. I know you must be hungry, and we won't be eating until at least four o'clock."

Jared refilled his mug. "No, baby, I've got everything I need right here." Pulling Holly in close, he began to nibble on her neck. A familiar warmth filled her. He knew right where her soft spot was, the one that caused her knees to go weak every time. She reached behind her and turned the burners off.

"Come with me," he whispered, leading her into the bedroom.

Holly woke up tangled in Jared's arms and legs. The drawn curtains gave the illusion of darkness, and for a moment Holly panicked. *The time!*

"Mmmm," Jared moaned as she twisted around to check the clock on her nightstand. They still needed to shower and dress before heading over to her parents' house. He pulled her back against his chest before she could get a peek at it. She kissed him lightly on the cheek and moved his arm off of her, trying to lift her body to sneak in another glance. It was one-thirty. They were fine.

"Holly," he said, this time with his eyes open. "You were amazing."

"I love you," she whispered back, smiling, "And you did okay for a hot shot."

"Well, I am a team leader now. That's kind of a big deal."

"You know, I've never slept with a team leader before. I have to say, you were pretty good."

"Pretty good? That's it? You just said I was amazing," he said with a teasing pout.

"No, *you* said *I* was amazing," she corrected. "I said you did okay." She took the covers and threw them over her head, knowing he would attack her with an onslaught of tickles at any moment.

After begging him to stop, admitting he was also truly amazing, and regaining her ability to breathe, she snuggled comfortably into the crook of his arm. Life was good.

"Great things are going to happen now, Hol. I can promise you that. I have big plans for us in the works."

"Really?" She propped herself up on one elbow and gently pushed Jared's hair off his forehead. *Ask me,* she commanded with her mind, *ask me right now.*

"It's true, baby," he continued. "I want you to be happy. It's the most important thing in the world to me. I'd do anything for you. In fact ..."

"What?" she asked, eyes wide. "What?"

"No, I don't want to spoil the surprise, but ... let's just say I'm working on something extra special for your birthday this year. If you're a good girl ... which in my book means being a little naughty," he teased with a gleam in his eyes.

Holly took a deep breath, smiling the widest, mischievous smile she could manage before wrapping her arms around him. "Oh, I can be naughty," she replied, tangling herself back up in her future fiancé's arms and legs. At least she hoped he would soon become her fiancé.

15

"So sorry we're late!" Holly burst through her parents' door, pulling Jared along by the hand. She stopped short to see everyone already finishing their dinner.

"It's cool," Tessa said, looking up from her plate. "It's not like Mom was slaving over a hot stove all day or anything."

"We're only a half-hour late. Why didn't you call me?"

"I'm afraid that's my fault," Patricia Haines said. "I invited some company over for dessert, and well, you know how I get. I wanted to make sure I'd have enough time to get everything cleaned up and put away before they got here. Tessa said she texted you.

Holly pulled out her phone.

Change of plans—we're eating at three. Mom's OCD strikes again. See you later. xo.

"Oh. I must have missed that one. We were kind of busy." What was meant to be a silent chuckle instead came out as a full-fledged giggle. Looking at Jared, she felt her cheeks turn red. Perhaps that was a little too much information in front of her parents. "Um, we were late because we stopped for this." She held up the bottle of wine they purchased on their way over to replace the bottle they drank earlier in the day.

"Well, aren't you two are all smiles," Tessa noted, taking the wine out of her hands and placing it on the table. "What's going on, eh?"

Patricia jumped up. "Sit," she ordered. "There's still plenty of food here. Help yourselves. You two look like you're about to burst at the seams. I'm guessing we have some celebrating to do. I'll get the corkscrew." She disappeared into the kitchen.

"We do have exciting news," Holly started, "but I'll wait until Mom is back."

"Tease!" Tessa said, sulking back into her seat.

"So, Jared," Bob Haines asked, ignoring his youngest daughter. "Did you see any of the game earlier? It was something."

"No, sir, I didn't get a chance to watch."

"Dad, weren't you listening? He and Holly were *busy* all afternoon," Tessa mocked.

Holly glared at her sister. She was lucky to be sitting too far away to be kicked under the table. She mouthed the words "troublemaker" instead. Tessa playfully blew a kiss back in response.

"It was a great game," he said, obviously trying to direct the conversation away from his daughters. "A little slow to start, but it really picked up toward the end."

"Here we are!" Patricia handed the corkscrew and the bottle of wine to her husband.

"Finally!" Tessa shrieked. "Apparently, the two love birds have news ... so? Spill it."

"Now, Tessa," her father said, clearly losing patience with his youngest child, "don't be pushy. Let's let them get settled in." He opened the bottle with a practiced ease and waited as everyone filled their glasses.

Patricia put her hands on Jared's shoulders. "I could tell the two of you had something exciting to tell us from the moment you walked in the door. You both are absolutely glowing! Why, I haven't seen a glow like that since Ava was pregnant with Jenna."

"Is that the big news?" Tessa asked, raising her eyebrows. "You better have a boy, or Dad may start disowning us." She put her arms up to her chest as if she were cradling a baby. "You know you shouldn't be drinking, Holly, right?"

"Tessa, slow down!" Holly demanded, trying to swallow her food. She glanced at Jared and noticed he was looking a bit pale, as was her father. She needed to do some serious back tracking ASAP before her not even yet fiancé changed his mind about proposing for her birthday. "Our *news* is that Jared got a big promotion and raise at work. You're now looking at Crestmont Memorial's newest Team Leader. He's moving up the ladder, and I couldn't be prouder." She tousled his hair and kissed him on the cheek before raising her glass in the air. "To Jared," she toasted.

"To Jared!" everyone repeated with enthusiasm, raising their glasses toward him.

Mostly everyone. Patricia no longer had her hands on his shoulders as she'd moved to stand by her husband. As she heard the news, her expression changed from ecstatic to happy, mixed with a smidge of disappointment. "Wonderful news," she said, obviously straining to maintain her smile, "just wonderful."

"Well done, son," Bob added, appearing extremely happy, and maybe a bit relieved in light of Tessa's little outburst. "When I started at the plastics plant, I was cleaning toilets. Within ten years I was managing the whole damn place. Hard work pays off. You've got a good head on your shoulders. Keep doing what you're doing, and we'll be celebrating promotions with you every year."

"Thank you," Jared said, grinning widely. He leaned into Holly with his arm around her shoulders. "I know this job is going to bring great things for Hol and me."

A knock at the door interrupted their celebration.

"Oh, that must be our company," Patricia said with a nervous tone. She glanced around the table at all the dishes and food still sitting out. "Oh," she repeated.

"It's okay, Mom," Holly said, standing up. "Everything looks fine. I'll let them in."

16

Holly walked over to the door as the visitors on the other side knocked one more time.

"Coming," she called out.

Swinging the door open with a welcoming grin on her face, she found herself face to face with Ben, an older couple who looked vaguely familiar from Ava's wedding, and a face she'd never forget—Michelle Floyd.

Michelle was tall, with long, silky black hair that curled perfectly in all the right places. She wore jeans that looked like they were painted on and a crisp white button down shirt with one button too many undone for Holly's taste. The white of her shirt matched the white of her teeth perfectly, which appeared even brighter with her impeccably painted red lips. No matter how many times Holly tried to wear red lipstick, she was never able to pull it off. This woman, however, managed it like a pro.

"Oh," she said, realizing it wasn't the most polite thing to say to guests coming to her parent's home, but it was the only thing she could manage.

Rushing to the door, Patricia ushered them in past Holly who was frozen in her spot. "Welcome. We're so glad you could stop over."

Ben smiled at Holly with kind eyes as he walked by, while Michelle barely looked at her.

"Girls," their mother began, "this is Shelley and Ed Oakes, their son Ben, and his girlfriend, um ... I'm sorry, tell me your name again."

"Michelle," she said, with a tone making it sound as if she received the greatest insult of her life.

"Yes, his girlfriend, Michelle," Patricia continued, either pretending not to notice her rude attitude or not care ... perhaps both.

"The Oakes' are Max's cousins. I thought it would be nice to have them over since we're practically family now, and Sunday is family dinner night. Isn't it funny? All these years in Forest Hills together, and we never ran into each other. These are my girls, Tessa and Holly."

Holly and Ben looked at each other and smiled. She wondered how long it would take their parents to figure out they went to the Soph Hop together in high school.

"We met Ben at Ava's wedding," Tessa offered.

"Oh, did you?" Patricia asked.

"Yes," Holly said. She tried not to sound too thrown off. Her heart raced as he continued to smile at her. "It's nice to see you again." As if in a trance, she continued to gaze into his eyes for a brief moment, forgetting everyone else around her ... until she felt the tug of Jared's hand.

"This is my boyfriend, Jared," she introduced. "I don't think you had a chance to meet at the wedding."

"No," Ben said, holding his arm out. "I don't believe we did."

Well, that's because he was already three sheets to the wind, she thought to herself. Of course, Ben already knew about Jared's embarrassing behavior that evening. Thankfully, he was discreet enough not to mention it.

"Nice to meet you," he said, shaking Ben's hand.

"It's nice to meet you also, Mr. and Mrs. Oakes," Holly added, "and hello, Michelle."

Michelle silently nodded and stood to the side while the rest of the guests said their hellos and made small talk. Holly and Tessa discreetly cleared away the dishes, leaving just her and Jared's half eaten meals.

"Please ... sit," Patricia finally offered when the table appeared presentable.

Clearing her throat with an obnoxious and loud sound, Michelle continued to stand as everyone else took their seats.

"Right," Ben said, standing back up, looking defeated. "I'm sorry to be rude, but I'm afraid we have to run already."

Holly's mother stood up again. "It's no problem, Ben. Your mom told me earlier you'd only be stopping in for a few minutes. She said you were going to a concert or something?"

"That's right. A band I like is playing at Farrell's Pub," Michelle said. Turning the corners of her lips up, she stared directly at Jared, bypassing Holly along the way. "You should come with us. You'd like them." Tilting her head, she wrapped a strand of her hair around her finger as she continued to stare at him.

Holly glared at her. *How would she know what Jared likes?*

"Thanks," Holly said, letting Michelle know that whatever invitation she extended to her boyfriend would also include herself. "But we just got here. We haven't even finished dinner."

"Aw, come on, Hol," Jared said, keeping his eyes on Michelle a moment longer than he should have before switching his attention back to his girlfriend. "It sounds fun. I don't think your parents would mind. Would you?" He glanced over to Patricia who only shook her head. "Besides, we need to celebrate."

Holly turned to her mother to try to get a read on the situation, but was unable to make eye contact. She sighed. "Are you sure it's okay, Mom? Dad?"

"Oh, it's fine," Bob said. "You don't need to hang out here with us old folks. Go and have fun."

"Well, in that case," Tessa said, getting up. "Would you two mind dropping me off at a party on your way out?"

Holly glared at Michelle again. In less than five minutes flat she'd managed to ruin her parent's family visit. She couldn't help but notice Ben didn't look happy about her actions either.

17

Holly and Jared dropped Tessa off and headed over to Farrell's Pub, which was surprisingly crowded for a Sunday. Most of the tables were filled, and the band had already started. Country. Jared hated country music. He was a rock 'n' roll guy through and through. Holly spotted Ben and Michelle in a corner U-shaped booth toward the back of the room.

"Sorry it took us so long, traffic was horrible," Holly said, as she walked up to them.

Ben stood as they arrived, but Michelle stayed in her seat, sipping some sort of fancy bottled water.

"It's no problem," he said. "I hope you don't mind, we ordered drinks for ourselves already."

He signaled for the waitress to come back around as Jared slid into the booth on the other side of Michelle, leaving Holly to sit on the end, directly across from Ben.

"Michelle," Ben started, "I forgot to mention Holly also went to high school with us. Do you remember her?"

"Holly? Hmm … no, I don't think so," Michelle stated, her tone making it clear she must not have been important enough to remember. She turned toward Jared and smiled. "And I know you weren't there. I would have remembered you."

He shook his head, eyes glued to her. "No, I didn't grow up in Forest Hills."

"Too bad," she said, curling her lips back.

Holly reached for his hand.

"Anyway," Michelle continued, switching back to Holly. "I mostly hung out with upper classmen or college kids. I found most of the kids in our class to be … I don't know … ordinary."

Holly looked at Michelle and had to resist the urge to roll her eyes. She tried to shake it off.

Ben turned his head toward his girlfriend. "If I recall, you had plenty of *friends* in our class."

Holly opened her eyes wide. *Did that mean what she thought it meant?*

"Oh sweetie, I didn't mean it like that," Michelle cooed, running her hand seductively across his chest.

"You know I had a crush on you from the minute I saw you in English class."

Yeah right. You didn't even know he existed. You were too busy hooking up with the football team ... and the basketball team.

"We never actually dated in high school. Or even spoke, really—" Ben started to tell the Holly, taking Michelle's hand off his chest and placing it back in her lap.

"But, thankfully, we found each other this summer," Michelle said, finishing his sentence.

When the waitress came by, Holly and Jared each ordered a beer and Michelle ordered another bottle of imported mineral water.

"I don't drink alcohol," she explained.

"So, Jared, I heard you mention you wanted to come out tonight to celebrate?" Ben asked.

Smiling, Holly slid in closer to her boyfriend. "Jared was promoted today," she announced, leaning into him.

"Here, here!" Ben called, lifting his bottle up. "Congratulations. What kind of work do you do?"

"As of today, I'm a Team Leader for the maintenance crew at Crestmont Memorial Hospital."

"Maintenance crew. That's like, what, janitorial?" Michelle asked, wrinkling her nose in disdain.

"No," Jared said. That question used to bother him, but he'd been asked it so many times now, he automatically responded with his standard answer.

"I'm in operations. We work on special projects, plus make sure all the hospital equipment is up to code and functioning properly."

It may not have bothered him, but it bothered Holly. Not the question itself, but the way Michelle had asked it. Just because she was some high-powered executive didn't give her the right to peer down her snooty nose at everyone else. What did Ben see in her anyway?

"Can't have a hospital with shoddy equipment, that's for sure," Ben stated. "They're lucky to have you leading their team."

"I'm not leading the *entire* team," Jared explained. "Right now, I'll have a group of about ten workers reporting to me."

"One day you might be," Holly told him, snuggling against his side.

"I see. Well, that does indeed sound like something to celebrate," Michelle said, losing a bit of her condescending tone. Twirling her hair again, she shifted her body a little closer to Jared's.

18

"Just water, please," Holly requested, when the waitress came by for the third time. Two beers on a mostly empty stomach had been one and a half too many for her.

"Another for me," Jared said, starting to sound a little tipsy.

"Don't you have to work the early shift tomorrow?" she asked, a sinking feeling in the pit of her stomach.

"It's cool, Hol. I'll be fine by morning," he replied, keeping his eyes on the waitress.

"Change mine to a cola, please," Holly said with a sigh. "Guess I'll need the caffeine to keep me awake to drive home."

"I'll have another." Michelle pointed to her empty bottle of Perrier.

"Cola sounds good for me, too, please," Ben said.

"Isn't this band fabulous?" Michelle asked as she swayed in place to the beat.

"It's awesome," Jared said, his eyes darting down her shirt more than they should be.

The waitress returned with the drinks. "Cheers," Michelle said, clinking her glass to Jared's bottle, while ignoring the rest of the table.

"Michelle?" Ben said, pointing to his watch. "It's getting late, and I've got to get up early for work tomorrow."

"Oh, sweetie, we haven't even danced yet. Come on, we have to at least dance."

"I'm not really in a dancing mood."

'How about you?" she asked, looking at Jared.

He smiled, eyes still on her chest, and nodded.

Sighing, Ben stood up to let them out.

He slid back in next to Holly where they watched as Michelle began gyrating against Jared who seemed oblivious and did his own odd chicken type dance.

"I'm sorry," Ben muttered to Holly.

She laughed under her breath. "This is a typical night out for me. You?"

"Pretty much," he said somberly.

After two songs, Ben walked up to Michelle, grabbed her elbow, and led her off the dance floor and back to the table. "We need to go."

Jared stumbled back behind them.

"Oh, sweetie," she said, kissing Ben on the cheek. "Can't we stay a little longer? It's so rare we get to go out like this, and Jared looks like he could use another beer."

She motioned for the waitress, and pointed to both their drinks, indicating they'd like refills, without bothering to ask if Ben or Holly wanted anything.

Hanging his head, Ben groaned. "Last one. Then I'm leaving—with or without you."

As Jared and Michelle sat back down, Holly noticed another button on her shirt had come undone, exposing even more of her cleavage. Twenty more minutes and she might actually wind up topless. Of course, this was Michelle Floyd. Apparently nothing really changed over the years.

Ben stood for a moment, trying to decide where he should sit, before sliding in next to Holly. Somehow, having him beside her made the situation seem not quite so bad. She could tell he was annoyed, as was she. Why did they keep putting up with this?

"Looks like you're the designated driver tonight," Ben said as the waitress brought Jared's beer.

Holly sighed. This was the first time they'd been out to a bar since Ava's wedding. She'd thought his binge drinking and flirting days were over. Apparently not.

"Cheers to us," she said to him, holding up her empty glass. It was a poor attempt to mock what was going on with their significant others.

"All hands on the table, kids," Ben called to Michelle and Jared.

"Oh, Benny," she replied with a playful grin, "we're just talking."

He smirked back. Even in sarcasm, he had a great smile.

"So how's the car?" Holly asked, trying to ignore the pair across from them.

Ben laughed. "I'm afraid it's dead. Didn't you get the notice for the memorial service?" He shook his head. "She served me well ... a sweet and respectable ride. A real class act." He glanced at his girlfriend. "Wish I could say the same about all of the women in my life."

Holly looked at Ben, not quite sure how to react. Was that a joke ... or not? She so wanted to laugh. In fact, she tried her hardest to hold it in, but the more she tried, the more trouble she had. Finally, a tiny giggle, which quickly escalated into louder chuckles, escaped. Ben followed with full on laughter.

"Yeah," Holly said, trying to catch her breath, "Mine's a broken down clunker, too." As they broke out into another round of uncontrollable laughter, she and Ben knocked heads.

"Hey, what's so funny over there?" Jared demanded, his words slurred.

"Yeah," Michelle added, closing one of her buttons and pulling her shirt up. "Let us in on the big joke."

"No. It's nothing," Ben said, regaining his composure. "We were talking cars."

"Well ..." Michelle muttered, glaring across the table. "I think I'm ready to go now, *my* love."

Ben got up and offered his hand to Holly to help her out of the booth. "It was a pleasure, as always," he said, before turning to Jared. "And very nice to finally meet you."

"Same to both of you," Holly replied for herself and Jared, who could barely stand, let alone speak a coherent sentence.

Michelle, as expected, didn't acknowledge Holly's words. Instead, she grabbed Ben's hand, tugging him toward the exit, before he had a chance to say anything more. Holly couldn't help but notice he pulled away from her long before they got to the door.

19

"How's this?" Dan stood up from his desk and walked to the space in front of his closed door so Holly could see him. He started moving his feet together and apart, in a really odd way, while clapping. The beat of the claps and the beat of the steps were completely out of sync. "Three plus three is six, but multiplied together is nine, isn't that just fine?"

"Hmmm," she said, trying not to laugh. Even in his most clumsy state, he was still completely adorable. "I'm not sure the timing works. How about: *The number three has a funky groove, multiply them together and watch them move. Three times three makes the number nine, just remember that, and you'll be fine.*"

"So much better," Dan replied, collapsing into the chair next to Holly. "I don't get how you come up with this stuff off the top of your head. You're amazing. It's no wonder all your students love you."

She put her hand up to her cheeks. "Stop, it's no big deal. My brain just likes to make silly rhymes."

"No, really. I've peeked in your doorway now and again to watch you teach. You have a way with children. That's not something you can learn in school, either. That's something that comes naturally. Not all teachers have it, but you do."

Holly looked at Dan. He was her boss and all, but she had no idea he'd been watching her, not like that. *Was it like that?* No, it was as a principal observing a teacher, that's all. He probably observed all of his co-workers. Yes—of course he did—it was his job as principal of the school.

"I'm sorry, I didn't mean to embarrass you. I'm just ... there's something about you I don't often see in educators. Something special. I wanted you to know."

Something special? The last time a guy told her there was something special about her, he was trying to convince her to take all of her clothes off. It had worked, too. She shut her eyes and tried to banish *that* thought from her mind. He was talking about teaching. She opened her eyes and glanced at the clock. It was four-thirty. Judging by the length of his previous meetings, time didn't really matter.

He smiled warmly. "Do you have kids of your own?"

"No," Holly replied, shying away.

"I'm sorry. I'm not supposed to ask questions like that. It's just—you'd be such a great mom."

"It's okay. I'm not married. Not that I need to be married to have kids or anything. I mean, I'd like to be married first, but it's not a requirement. There are lots of great single moms out there. In fact, they're probably even better at parenting because they have to work twice as hard at what they do. Of course, married moms are hardworking, too. They've got a lot on their shoulders as well. I wasn't implying they had it easy or anything." *Stop babbling, Holly!* "Anyway, I hope to have kids one day. I guess that was more info than you were asking for." She felt her cheeks get even hotter.

"I appreciate your honesty." He probably regretted asking the question at this point. "Oh, hey, didn't you want to show me dance moves or something?"

"Uh … sure." Flustered, she got up and faced him, feeling self-conscious. "Well, um, I was thinking something like this."

Moving her arms and legs in a slow, rhythmic motion, she began counting to the same beat the rap followed.

Dan got up out of his chair and stood next to her. Swinging his arms first, he followed her. "Like this?"

She smiled. It needed work—a lot of work—but at least he was moving to the right beat this time.

"That's right. Now try it with the legs."

Keeping the arms going, he moved his left foot forward, then back. He then moved his right foot forward and back. Holly watched as he struggled, but miraculously appeared to be keeping up ... in a strange, choppy sort of way.

"Ah ha ha!" Dan exclaimed, seeming to be quite pleased with himself. "I think I've got it!"

"Great," Holly said, sharing his enthusiasm, while trying not to laugh at his awkward style.

He repeated the sequence one more time, then added in an odd shoulder wave Holly hadn't ever seen before. It was sort of a mixture between a shimmy and a shake. Whatever it was, it wasn't good. It threw his balance off, and when he tried to catch himself, he hooked Holly's foot with his own. She felt the fall coming, but was unable to control it. Apparently Dan couldn't control his either, as within seconds, he was directly on top of her ... their faces only inches apart.

She could feel his breath quickening as he looked into her eyes and felt her own chest rise and fall as she tried to steady her own breathing. There were only two ways this scenario could end: either he would get up, or he would kiss her. He did neither. Why was he just lying on top of her, staring into her eyes?

"What's going on in here?"

Or make that three scenarios ... Elaine Fairview could walk in.

"Mrs. Fairview!" Dan said, scurrying to his feet. He brushed invisible dust off his pants before offering Holly a hand to help her up. "Ms. Haines and I were practicing our routine ... for the talent show. We're doing a rap ... er ... a song."

"And a dance," Holly interjected.

"I see," Elaine said, crossing her arms over her chest.

"Well, it seems I have two left feet, and I tripped is all, taking poor Ms. Haines down with me. Luckily, we still have over a month to figure it all out. So, um, what can I do for you, Mrs. Fairview?"

"I was stopping by to see if you had a few minutes to discuss changes I'd like to make to the spring curriculum. That is, if you don't mind taking a break from singing and dancing to talk about something of substance."

"I need to get going anyway," Holly said, grabbing her coat and bag. "You keep practicing, Dan. Same time next week?"

"Sounds great," he replied, grimacing. He appeared to have a *please don't leave me alone with this old hag* expression on his face.

"Nice to see you again, Mrs. Fairview," Holly called out as she left the office, laughing to herself as she headed down the hall and out to her car.

20

"What are you doing home so early? Are you sick?"

Setting her briefcase and purse down inside the door, Holly walked over to the couch to sit on the edge beside Jared, who was lying down. She was still smiling, thinking about the look on Elaine's face when she walked in on her and Dan. It must have been quite a sight—her on the floor with the principal on top of her.

"My boss sent me home early," he mumbled. "I had a rough day."

"What do you mean?" She glanced at the coffee table where a six-pack of beer sat—well, six minus three—one of which was still in Jared's hand. She bent down to pick up the metal tops and empty bottles that littered the floor.

"One of the guys on my crew was giving me a hard time. Not listening, talking back, and stuff. I guess he's not used to having me as his boss now or something, I don't know. We got into it a little. He started cursing at me, and I got pissed, so I shoved him. He's the one who started throwing punches. I was only defending myself after that."

"You got into a fight?" Holly asked, finally noticing Jared's swollen lip. "You can't do stuff like that at work. You'll get fired! You didn't, did you?"

"No, I didn't. But thanks for backing me up, babe. I appreciate the support." He finished his beer, threw the bottle on the floor, and grabbed a fourth, tossing the top on the floor as well.

She sighed and stood up. "Well, are you okay? Can I get you some ice?"

"Don't bother." He turned his head away from her and stared up at the ceiling.

"What did your boss say?" she asked. "Did the other guy get in trouble at least?"

"Yeah, we both got written up. It's no big deal."

"No big deal? Getting written up *is* a big deal! You were just promoted. Now is the time when everyone is watching you."

Jared slammed his bottle down on the coffee table, spilling beer on the newspaper sitting next to it.

"Jesus, Holly, give me a freaking break. So I made one mistake. Why don't you get off my case for once and leave me alone?"

She stood up and stared at him for a moment as his hurtful words sunk in. "Gladly," she said, quietly, coldly, as she reached down to grab her purse. "I'm going to my parents. There are leftovers in the fridge in case you're interested in something other than liquids for dinner. One other thing, don't ever think that I don't support you, because I do, more than anybody else in this world. If I didn't, I wouldn't give a damn about what happened to you at work today." She opened the door to the apartment and turned around before walking into the hallway. "Oh, and my day was great, thanks for asking ... as usual."

"Mom? Dad?" Holly called out as she walked through the door. She'd wanted to call them on the way there to let them know she was coming over, but her phone was still in her briefcase back at her apartment. After making such a grand departure, she hadn't felt like going back to get it. Her exits weren't always that perfect. Returning for something would have killed the effect. Not that Jared would remember her words three beers in, but still, it was satisfying at the very least.

"They're in the kitchen."

She turned toward the familiar voice coming from the couch.

"Ben?" she asked, startled. "What? Why? I'm sorry, that was rude. I mean, hi. I wasn't expecting to see you."

He put down the magazine he'd been reading and stood up.

"Holly?" Patricia called out, entering the living room. "Is everything all right, sweetie? What are you doing here?"

"I'm fine," she lied, giving her mom a kiss on the cheek. "Jared isn't feeling well, so I wanted to get out of the house." *It was sort of true.*

"It's no problem. You know you're always welcome here. Is it the flu?"

"No, he's just a little under the weather." She glanced at Ben and back at her mother. "I didn't realize you had company," she said, trying to figure out what was going on.

"Oh, I invited Shelley and Ed over again. We had such a lovely evening the last time they were here. Did you know you and Ben went to the Soph Hop together? Well of course you did. You'll never believe what I found going through some old albums." She pulled the picture of them in their yellow frilly outfits out of her apron pocket.

"We really do need to destroy all copies of that photo," Holly told Ben.

"Ben here has been so sweet. He came along to help your dad fix something in the garage. You know how he is ... always wanting to tackle the hard jobs himself when he can get some help. Not that you and your sisters aren't helpful, of course."

"It's okay, Mom. It's no secret our father always wanted a boy."

"Oh, stop. He loves you girls, and you know it. You three just never seemed interested in any of his fix-it stuff, although he did give it a good try there for a while. Remember that Christmas when he bought you all tool belts?"

Holly laughed. "Tessa used hers as a Barbie carrier. Clever when you think about it. Then Ava and I followed her lead and used ours for make-up and hair accessories."

"That's right. I'd forgotten about that. I think that was the point where he finally came to terms with the fact that you were all girly girls. Anyway, he needed a little help, and ... well, he's not getting any younger, you know. I guess with Max all the way across the country, he figured maybe Ben could help out."

"Jared's here, too," she reminded her.

"Right," Patricia said with a forced grin. "Well, poor Ben is probably bored now that all of us old folks have congregated in the kitchen. You know how that goes. I told you that you could watch TV," she reminded him.

"It's okay," he replied. He held up the magazine that had been sitting out on the coffee table for the past year and said, "I've been catching up on my reading."

Holly's mom smiled at him and turned back to her daughter. "Anyway, I'm sure he's glad you're here now. Why don't you take him down to the rec room in the basement. You two can play ping pong until dinner's ready."

"Or we can shoot pool," Holly suggested with a twinkle in her eye.

"Holly," she warned, giving her the stern look she'd perfected from her two decades of mothering.

"I'll go easy," she assured her, before nodding at Ben. "You interested?"

He shrugged. "Sure. Why not?"

21

"So this was a surprise," Holly said as she racked up the balls.

"For me, too," Ben replied. "I wasn't expecting to see you here. Your parents said you weren't coming."

"You asked?" She looked up and noticed his face was a little flushed.

"Well, yes. I was curious … to know if you *and* Jared would be here … so I'd have someone to talk to. It's never fun coming to these things and being the odd man out. Did I hear you say Jared was sick?"

"Sick?" Holly repeated. "Oh … yes." She'd nearly forgotten that was the excuse she'd used. "It's nothing serious, but you know, since I'm around kids all day at school, I didn't want to catch anything I could pass along." She really needed to work on her rambling thing.

"That makes sense. Anyway, I'm glad I wound up coming. I wasn't going to, but then my mom said your dad needed help with something, so here I am." Ben smiled and tilted his head as he gazed at her.

Was he flirting, or was her mind playing tricks on her? No, it must just be because she was angry with Jared. Or ...was Tessa right? Did fate keep pushing them together? Holly couldn't help but stare into his eyes, searching for some sort of a sign.

"Looks like you've got everything set up," he said, bringing her out of her thoughts.

"What? Right." She handed him the coin they always kept on the edge of the table. "Heads or tails?"

"Ladies first, I insist."

Holly positioned her stick and made a clean break. She could swear she caught Ben's eyes wandering from the pool table to her body as she leaned over the table.

"Three ball in the side pocket," she said, leaning over more than was strictly necessary. Well maybe he wasn't flirting, but that didn't mean she couldn't. What harm would it do?

"Nice," Ben said when the ball rolled neatly into the hole.

He was talking about the shot ... wasn't he? Holly moved to the other side. She continued to hit ball after ball into their intended pockets as Ben watched.

Finally, feeling she had showed off enough, she purposely missed. "You're up," she said.

"Wow. This is taking it easy on me?"

Smiling, Holly shrugged.

Ben picked out a stick from the wall and proceeded to turn it into the chalk block, getting blue powder all over his hands. Walking over to the table, he awkwardly positioned the stick along his arm.

"Um, seven-ball in that far hole on the left." He moved the cue ball in front of the seven and slid the pool stick back between his fingers. As the pole came forward, it lurched up and sideways, completely missing the ball. Instead, another ball bounced off the table.

Putting her hand to her mouth, Holly tried to hide her laughter. "So, you play this game often?" she asked with a hint of sarcasm.

"Never played before in my life," he admitted with an adorable sheepish grin. "That obvious?"

She nodded, biting her lower lip. She needed to stop letting his smiles affect her. "The first giveaway was when you tried to pocket one of my balls. I'm solids, you're stripes." She pointed to the remaining balls on the table. "Your blue fingers were another good hint, followed by your remarkable form. In fact, I've never seen anything like it." She giggled again, this time without trying to hide it.

"And I thought I'd be a natural," he said, laughing along with her.

"Here, let me show you." Coming up behind him, she positioned her hands over his, showing him how to gently glide the pole between his fingers—back and forth in a rhythmic motion. Holly closed her eyes, taking in his clean scent. She felt his muscular body lean into hers, his warmth radiating against her.

"Would you kids like a drink?" Patricia asked, coming down the stairs with a couple of bottles of soda. They broke apart quickly.

"Great," Ben said, rushing over to take the beverages from her. "Holly was just trying to show me how to play this game, but it seems I'm a lost cause."

Her mom smiled, her expression full of pity. "I'm afraid even the most experienced players don't stand a chance against my lovely daughter. Anyway, dinner should be ready in about fifteen minutes." She headed back up the steps.

Holly and Ben sat with their drinks on the old, ratty couch that had been in the basement for the last twenty years.

"I probably should have warned you," she said with a shameless grin. "I've been undefeated for three years now."

"Impressive."

"It's turned into a running joke in the house. When a new person comes in, they get sent to the basement to play pool against me ... an initiation of sorts."

"An initiation I failed miserably at," Ben agreed, though he didn't sound too heartbroken over it.

Holly chuckled and nodded. "You and so many others. My mom tried to save you by suggesting ping pong. Now you know why."

"Is there any way to redeem myself?" he asked playfully.

"Nope, I am the merciless Queen Holly. You are now part of my royal billiards kingdom."

Ben slid off the couch and bowed down at Holly's feet

"You may sit, my loyal subject," she said with a flirty smile.

They took sips of their drinks to fill the silence that suddenly hung heavily in the air.

"You seem like you would be a really fun teacher," Ben finally said.

"Oh," Holly murmured, caught off guard. "I don't know about that. We try to have a good time. Math can be a pretty dry subject sometimes. I'm lucky I have a great group of kids this year."

"It must take a lot of patience though, having to be around children all day."

She shrugged. "I don't really think about it like that. It doesn't feel like work most of the time. I guess I've always loved kids. I can't wait until I have a houseful of my own."

"What about Jared? Does he want children, too?"

Holly looked down. Sure, she and Jared had talked about having a family, but each time he said he wanted them, he sounded less than enthusiastic. Of course, none of that would even happen until he actually proposed. He'd told her on more than one occasion that having children before they were married was out of the question.

"I'm sorry, am I getting too personal?" Ben asked, putting his drink down on the side table.

"No, it's fine. Jared wants kids, just not quite the brood I'm hoping for. What about you and Michelle?"

Ben sighed and ran his fingers through his hair.

"Now I'm getting too personal," she said.

"It's okay." He cupped his hands in his face for a moment and looked at Holly. "We ... broke up."

"Oh," she said, not sure how to respond. "I ... I'm sorry."

"Thanks," Ben said, managing a smile. "It's okay. I'm the one who broke up with her. It wasn't working out anymore. It happened the night we saw you. After we left the pub. I was tired of her behavior."

"I understand," she said, "I don't know why I put up with it from Jared. The flirting really gets old after a while.

"That was only a small part of it."

"So what set you over the edge?"

"It was the way she spoke to your parents—and to you. I couldn't deal with her complete lack of respect toward someone I—" He stopped abruptly and looked down.

"What?" she asked.

Focusing back to Holly, he smiled. "I— I was just going to say toward someone who is one of my friends."

She nodded and smiled back. "Well, I am sorry. It's never easy having to break up, no matter what the circumstances."

"Thanks. I actually feel like a huge weight's been lifted off my shoulders. Believe it or not, she was pretty high maintenance."

"You don't say," Holly said, trying not to roll her eyes. "How did she take it?"

"Not great. I was kind of surprised at her reaction, since she never seemed like the kind of girl who would want to be tied down to one guy. It was probably just for show. I have a feeling she'll be over me before the weekend's out. We didn't want the same things out of life anyway, and a relationship built on values that don't match is doomed right from the start."

Holly stared at him as his words sank in, letting them run through her mind a second time.

"Anyway, I'm going on and on here," he continued. "How are things with you and Jared?"

She closed her eyes and shook her head, trying to hold back the tears as they started to form. It would have been so easy for her to say "fine" and move the conversation to another subject. Why did that one simple question make her so emotional? Was it the fight this evening, what Ben just said about incompatible values, or their entire situation?

She quickly wiped away the tears that managed to escape. "I didn't mean to cry," she whispered. "It's been a really frustrating time for me."

Looking at Holly, Ben held her gaze in a way that took her back to their sophomore dance. He reached over, wiping the tears she'd missed, letting his hand rest on her cheek. She tilted her head as he leaned in to tenderly kiss her lips.

"Dinner!" Patricia called from the top of the stairs.

"I'm so sorry," he said, pulling away. "I never should have—"

"No," Holly stated, interrupting him. "It was my fault."

"I ... I should really go." He ran up the steps.

Stunned, Holly sat on the couch, listening as she overheard Ben make up an excuse about getting a call regarding an emergency at the plant. She waited, listening to the sounds of the front door slamming shut, followed by a car racing down the driveway, before heading upstairs.

22

"Tessa says she thinks it's fate that we keep bumping into each other. Do you think that's true?" Holly sat in the makeshift office she and Jared had set up in the spare bedroom of their apartment doodling hearts in the corner of her memo pad while she talked to Ava on the phone. She always doodled while trying to figure out a problem. It was a habit she'd had since she was a little girl. Not that Ben was a problem. She just hadn't been able to get him off her mind since the kiss last night.

After Ben ran out, Holly decided she needed to go home and try to salvage what was left of her own relationship with Jared. Making the excuse her boyfriend needed her to pick up some medicine for his *illness*, she said goodbye to her parents and their company before they could convince her to stay for dinner. When she got back to her apartment, she could smell the garlic and basil before even opening the front door. Walking in she noticed the unopened beers were still in their carton and the almost full beer bottle that Jared had opened right before she'd stormed out, was still on the coffee table. Continuing into the kitchen she found him washing pots from the dinner he'd prepared. Two plates piled high with pasta sat on the kitchen table along with a loaf of garlic bread and two candlesticks waiting to be lit. A romantic dinner. That seemed to be his way of apologizing lately.

"What do *you* think?" Ava asked. "Do *you* think it's fate?"

"I think I was mad at Jared, and I got caught up in the moment?" Holly said with an uncertain tone.

"Are you asking me or telling me?"

"I'm giving you the answer I'm supposed to give— the one that's the most rational. It's the answer that says I've invested three years of my life with Jared, and yeah, he messes up here and there, but he does love me, and he's hinted he's getting ready to settle down and start a family. It's the answer that says I've only seen Ben a handful of times, and what I'm feeling can't be anything more than a leftover high school crush."

Holly put down her pen and walked to the kitchen to heat up her dinner—leftover pasta from the night before.

"Okay, so you gave me the most rational answer. Now what's the real answer?" Ava asked.

She took her plate out of the microwave, sat at the kitchen table, and sighed.

"The real answer is I can't stop thinking about Ben *and* the kiss ..."

Twirling her fork in her pasta, she stared at the red and white swirls on her plate. Why *was* she still thinking about the kiss? She and Jared had made up over dinner last night, which then carried over into the bedroom. That's what she *should* be thinking about.

"At least he broke up with that woman. I heard she was— just a— I don't know."

Holly laughed. "A bitch?"

"Yes, a total bitch," Ava agreed. "Tessa told me how she acted at Mom and Dad's house."

Holly chuckled again. "I thought maybe I was being a little too judgmental because of what she was like in high school. But I'm glad Tessa noticed, too. Let me tell you, it was so hard to be civil to her the night we all went out. I wanted to smack her upside the head. It's a good thing our youngest sister wasn't with us. She definitely would have told her where to stick it. The only reason I was being the slightest bit polite was because Ben is Max's cousin. You know, that whole family thing. I thought you all might be friends."

"Nope, we never met her. And I hope we never do," Ava said.

"Anyway, her character is completely irrelevant now that she's out of the picture. We'll never have to deal with her again, thank goodness." Holly shuddered at the thought of her. "It's just—it was easier not to think about Ben when I thought he was unavailable."

"So now what?" Ava asked.

"It's like I said before, I have Jared, and he did redeem himself after our big fight. I know you all don't think he's the best choice for me, but he's not always a loser. He really can be a sweet guy."

"Nobody thinks he's a loser, Holly. We just want you to be happy. If Jared is capable of getting his act together and giving you everything you want, then more power to him. He's already scored major points with his raise and promotion. And I'm glad he had a nice dinner and apology waiting for you when you got home last night."

Holly nodded to herself. If all of that was true, then why couldn't she stop thinking about Ben?

23

"Your brother-in-law told me where you worked," Ben said as he leaned up against his car.

Holly stopped in her tracks as she walked out of the school building with Dan at six o'clock. They'd been working on their routine for the talent show, and since it had gotten so late, they'd agreed to grab a bite to eat together. She knew Jared was working the late shift and wouldn't be home for hours.

"Perhaps a rain check?" Dan said, looking from Holly to Ben.

"Are you sure?" she asked.

"It's no problem. I've got a ton of work to catch up on anyway. We made great progress tonight." He moved his feet perfectly in sync with the dance steps Holly had taught him that afternoon and put two thumbs up.

"Looks great. I'll see you tomorrow." She smiled as she watched him walk to his car.

"Sorry, I didn't mean to interrupt."

"How long have you been out here?" Holly asked.

"I don't know, since about four-thirty, I guess. That's what time you normally leave, right?"

"Normally, yes. What are you doing here?" *He sat out here for an hour and a half?*

"I was hoping I could talk to you."

"Sure," she said, although she wasn't certain she really wanted to have this conversation. It was bound to be awkward. "What's up?"

He glanced around. "Do you think we could go somewhere private?"

Against her better judgment, she replied, "Jared's working the late shift, and I've got leftover chili at my place. I'm only a few blocks away if you want to follow me over."

He nodded, getting back into his car.

Holly went in first to make certain Jared really *was* working the late shift and hadn't been sent home early again. She sighed in relief as she stepped into the empty apartment, wondering what she would have told Jared about having Ben in tow.

"Nice place," he said.

"Thanks." It was pretty nice. They were lucky to get the three bedroom rent-controlled apartment passed down from Jared's grandmother.

"Here, let me take your coat."

As he pulled his jacket off, the top two buttons on his shirt came undone. Holly watched the material slide across Ben's muscular chest. She blinked her eyes and turned away, banishing the thought of the rest of the shirt falling away from his body. By the time she hung up his coat, his shirt was back in place and fully buttoned.

"I–I'll get d–dinner started," she stammered, trying to regain her composure. "Would you like a drink?" She desperately wanted to open a window to let in a bit of cool air. Instead, she stuck her head in the refrigerator as she reached in for the chili.

"Water would be great."

"How's the new car?" she asked, trying to make small talk to take her mind off of what she had just seen. Maybe coming back to her apartment wasn't such a good idea after all.

"It's great," he responded. "Very reliable."

"So ... you wanted to talk to me?" She handed him his glass and put the chili on the stove. "Please ..."

Motioning to the couch in the living room, she made sure to leave ample space between them as she sat down. She didn't want to risk another episode like the one she just experienced.

Ben took a long drink before speaking. "I shouldn't have run out like that the other day. I feel bad about it ... guilty is really the better word. It's been bothering me since it happened. Not about the kiss, about running out. It was kind of a weird thing to do. I guess I didn't know what to do, you know?"

Holly nodded. *So he didn't feel guilty about the kiss part?* "The whole thing was so unexpected," she said. "And probably shouldn't have happened. I was upset with Jared, but that didn't mean I should be kissing other men."

"Right. The thing is—"

The timer on the stove buzzed.

"Hold that thought," Holly said, getting up. "This stuff heats up really fast, I don't want it to burn." She let out a breath as she walked to the kitchen. The conversation was taking an odd turn—her chili had impeccable timing.

Ben seemed nervous as she handed him a bowl of piping hot food. "Thanks. It looks and smells great."

Taking her seat next to him, she placed her own bowl on the coffee table. "You were saying?"

"I was saying ... yes," he repeated, as if he needed a reminder of where he left off. He balanced the bowl on his leg, staring at his food, while stirring raptly as if all of the answers were in there. "Well, the thing is," he paused again. "You know how at the wedding I told you I wasn't really good about the whole talking to women thing back in high school?" he asked with an uneasy laugh. "I guess I'm still not very good."

"You're doing okay," she lied.

"I'm not, but thanks. Anyway, ever since we saw each other at the wedding, I — I know we shouldn't have, but I'm glad we kissed. I needed to know. I felt something—when we kissed, that is." He searched her eyes. "Did you feel it too?"

Holly nodded and sighed. "But—we can't. I can't."

"I know. I just haven't been able to stop thinking about—"

The phone in the kitchen began to ring interrupting him. *Jared.* It was a sign. It had to be.

"I have to get that." She ran into the kitchen. Taking the receiver into the bedroom, she softly closed the door behind her as she said, "Hello?"

"Hey baby. I'm just checking in to say hi. These long shifts are killing me. I can't wait to get home and wrap my arms around you."

Holly closed her eyes and leaned against the wall. "How's work going?" she asked.

"Oh, you know … same old boring crap. The guys aren't giving me shit anymore at least. Now I have to get my boss off my back. He's been in a bad mood all night. Anyway, my break's just about over. I'll be home around midnight."

"I'll leave dinner for you in the stove."

"Thanks, baby," he said, and then yelled to someone else, "I'm coming! Geez—can't a guy get thirty seconds to take a piss?" He swiftly hung up the phone.

Holly closed her eyes for a moment, trying to think of the right words to say to Ben, before walking back into the living room. When she got there, he was already gone. Next to his bowl of chili was a scribbled note that read, "*I'm sorry.*"

24

"**A**re you okay? You don't seem your normal cheerful self." Dan looked over at Holly as they ran through the first several lines of their rap. Her performance was lackluster at best.

"What?" she responded. "Yes, yes, I'm fine. I've just got a lot on my mind, sorry. We can do it again if you want."

"It's okay. I know how busy it gets around here trying to get everything done with the short week for Thanksgiving. We probably should've skipped rehearsal today."

She wished she could concentrate on the talent show and forget about everything else. Things with

Jared were fine. Great actually. He hadn't had any more problems at work or drunken incidents since he apologized and had made a few more hints about a big surprise coming her way for her birthday. Something shiny that was guaranteed to make her smile. If only she could forget about ...

"So what do you say?" Dan asked. "Should we call it for today and pick up after the holiday? We'll still have plenty of time to finish. You seem kind of beat. No offense."

Holly laughed. "None taken. But I'd rather stay, if that's all right. The stuff that's got me stressed out isn't work related." She knew Jared wouldn't be back until around eight o'clock. The last thing she wanted to do was go home to a quiet, empty apartment where her mind would surely wander to places she wanted to keep tucked away. Right now she only wanted to keep busy.

"I hear you. My family's been giving me a lot of pressure lately, too. Happens every year around this time. *Why can't you be more like your brothers and settle down with a family?* Gotta love the holidays! Ho, ho, ho, and pass the rum."

"How many brothers do you have?" she asked.

"Two. I'm the youngest, and they're both married with two kids each. Apparently for me, having five hundred kids nine months out of the year doesn't count."

"I feel your pain," she said, nodding. "I've got two sisters. My older one is married with a kid. I'm in the middle, and my younger sister is still in college, so that makes me next in line. The pressure is full on."

"Fun, isn't it? New plan. We'll still pick this up after the break, but instead of going home, let's go grab that bite we never had a chance to get. Didn't we agree on a rain check?"

Holly smiled. "As a matter of fact, we did."

"Listen," Dan said. "I need to tell you something before we go. Something I've been wanting to tell you for a while now." Staring intensely into her eyes, he placed his hands on her shoulder and tilted his head.

Oh my God. He's going to kiss me. I'm in my boss's office, and he's going to kiss me. She needed to stop him, she just couldn't get the words out—she was completely frozen in shock at what was about to happen.

"Am I too early?"

Holly tore her eyes away from Dan to follow the sound of the voice. Before her stood a totally hot guy with dark blonde wavy hair and chiseled features. She could see the ripples of his muscles under his tight shirt. What was with all these guys who looked like underwear models?

"Oh, hello. No, you're not too early at all. In fact your timing is perfect." Dan tightened his grip on her shoulders as he faced the other man and said, "Holly, I'd like you to meet my partner, Alex."

"Ah, Holly," the man said, flashing a radiating smile. "It's great to finally meet you. Dan talks about you all the time."

"Thanks. It's nice to meet you, too." She turned back to Dan. "So ... your ... partner?" she asked, looking between the two men with a confused expression. "Like business partner? For what, the talent show?"

Dan released Holly's shoulders and walked over to Alex, taking his hand. "No, partner as in life partner."

Holly's chin dropped, as she peered at him. "You mean ... you're gay?"

He raised his eyebrows and nodded. "That's what I was about to tell you. And also I wanted to let you know Alex would be joining us. I had asked him to stop by to watch us rehearse. I thought it might be good for us to get comfortable performing in front of someone. But we can start that part next time. Mind if Alex tags along for dinner?"

"Wow," Holly said, raising her eyebrows. "Ok. Sure, Dan, whatever you'd like." She shook her head and laughed under her breath. "I seriously have to work on reading signals better. I thought for sure you were flirting with me today ... and for the past couple of months. In fact, I could have sworn you were about to kiss me."

"Really?" Alex asked, half chuckling, looking at his boyfriend.

"What?" Dan asked. "Could happen. I'm cute and loveable."

"Yes," Alex said, kissing him on the cheek, playfully. "Of course you are. Holly's just a little too feminine for you, that's all."

"It's true," Dan agreed.

She laughed. "It's okay. I'm taken anyway. I'm just usually spot on about these things." She shook her head again. "Wow, okay. Well, it's nice to meet you, Alex. Has anyone told you the two of you make a *really* good looking couple?"

Alex nudged Dan in the shoulder, and smiled. "Thanks. Hey, did someone say something about food?"

The tiny diner on the other side of town had only one table open.

"Where'd you find this place? I had no idea this even existed," Holly said, checking out her surroundings.

"It only opened a couple of months ago," Dan explained as they sat down. "It received a big write-up in the city paper. We've been dying to come here. Usually the line is out the door. I figured it wouldn't be so bad at four o'clock on a Wednesday. Looks like we got lucky."

She scanned the menu. "So what's good?"

"Milkshakes," Alex said. "People come from miles around to get their hands on one."

"Ah, so you've heard I've been known to have ice cream for dinner every now and again?"

"You, too?" Dan asked. "That's one of our standard meals. Their roast beef sandwich is supposed to be very good as well. Actually, I don't think you can go wrong with anything here."

They all ordered sandwiches and chocolate shakes. When the waitress brought them over, Holly's eyes nearly popped out of her head.

"This is for one person?" she asked. "Guess I know what I'll be having for lunch tomorrow and dinner … and possibly lunch the next day." Taking a sip of her milkshake, she sat back in her chair. "Oh, I have died and gone to heaven. This is orgasmic. Oh shit. Did I just say *orgasmic* in front of my boss? … Did I just say *shit* in front of my boss?" Holly put her hands over her eyes like a visor and sunk into her seat, feeling her cheeks turn what was surely a shade of crimson.

Dan cracked up. "I can't believe we haven't done this before. The three of us need to hang out more often. Don't you think, Alex?"

"Absolutely," he said, laughing also. "Holly is just adorable."

"See?" Dan said, looking at her. "This is exactly what we needed, I can feel the stress easing already."

He took a sip of his shake and leaned back into his chair. Closing his eyes, he started to moan.

Oh ... he wasn't ...

"Holly."

Dan opened his eyes as Holly looked over to the familiar male voice.

"Ben ... hi." She hadn't seen him since that awkward night in her apartment. She sat in silence for a moment as she tried to think of something to say over the pounding of her heart. "I'm sorry, this is Dan Harper, the principal at the school where I teach, and his partner, Alex—" She realized she never got his last name.

"Schiff," he said, standing up to shake Ben's hand.

Dan stood up as well. "It's nice to see you again. We didn't get a chance to meet the other day."

"Right, I'm sorry if I interrupted something then when I showed up at school," he said with an odd sadness to his voice.

"Oh no, it was fine. We were wrapping up a staff meeting." Dan looked around their tiny table that was already packed with food. "Would you like to join us?"

Holly glanced away briefly. The three of them had been having such a wonderful stress-free meal. Dan didn't know. He was only being polite. As far as he was concerned, Ben was one of Holly's friends. *And he still was—but he was more than that.* She met Ben's eyes. He appeared so ... lost. She wanted to reach out to him. She just ... couldn't.

"No, but thank you," he said, with an uncomfortable tone. Maybe she had been reading him wrong after all. Maybe what she interpreted as sadness was really him being distant and distracted. "I think I see a stool at the counter opening up. It was nice to meet you both ... and Holly," he said with a certain formality, "it was nice to see you again."

"You too," Holly said quietly. Her phone buzzed as they watched him walk away.

"Is everything okay?" Dan asked. "You seemed kind of thrown off when he came over."

"No, everything's fine." She sighed and read her text message.

Hey baby. I'm going to be a little late tonight. We got our holiday bonus early. Have some shopping to do for my sweetie's special surprise. The future is looking awesome for us—you & me, baby! You & me. xoxo.

She shook her head. She was an idiot. Why was she sitting here getting upset about Ben, when she had the perfect guy at home?

25

"Happy Birthday, baby." Jared rolled over and kissed Holly, lightly stroking her hair as he nuzzled her neck.

"Mmmm," she moaned, curling into him. "It's not my birthday, silly, it's Thanksgiving. My birthday is still two weeks away."

He still knew exactly how to send a shiver up her spine the first thing in the morning. It helped he'd been hinting daily he had something exciting planned for her birthday. Did this mean he was giving it to her early? She perked up.

"I know baby, but since I got my bonus already, I was able to pick up your big surprise sooner than I expected. Of course, if you don't want it—" He rolled away from her, pretending to be upset.

"What?" she asked with a wide smile. "No, it's okay. You can give it to me early. I mean, if that's what you want to do. She playfully nipped at his shoulders, trying to get him to come back.

"I don't know," he said, "I may need a little convincing." He turned his head toward her, flashing a mischievous grin. "Just how deserving are you?"

"Oh, I'm very deserving," Holly said, wrapping her body around him. "Would you like me to show you?"

An hour and a half later, Holly woke up alone in bed. "Jared?" she called out.

"In the kitchen," he replied.

She threw on her robe and followed the smell of freshly brewed coffee. Kissing him on the cheek, she sat down at the table as he poured her a cup.

"What time are we going over to your parents?" he asked, smiling the biggest smile she'd seen in weeks.

Normally they'd head over around four o'clock, but since Ava, Max, and Jenna were coming in, she wanted to get there early to visit and share her news. This was going to be a year to remember.

"I guess we'll leave as soon as we get dressed," Holly said. "So …" Grabbing her mug, she walked over to Jared.

"So…" he repeated. "Why don't you go make yourself pretty, and when you get back, I'll have your surprise waiting for you. Then we can go see your family."

Beaming, she kissed him before racing off to take the quickest shower she'd ever taken in her entire life. When she returned, she noticed a small box with a blue bow sitting on the coffee table. Walking over to the couch, she sat down beside Jared and waited.

"Happy Birthday, babe!" he finally said, handing the gift to her.

Holly stared at him. It wasn't exactly the proposal she was expecting, but maybe he was saving the good stuff for after she saw the ring. She slowly opened the box, wanting to savor the moment she'd been waiting so long for. She knew he didn't have a lot of money, and she didn't have great expectations. The ring part wasn't even that important to her. It was the message and commitment behind it.

"Well?" Jared asked as Holly just sat there staring, not saying a word.

"It's a key," she finally said. *A key. Not a ring ... a key.*

"I know, silly." He gave her a quick kiss on the lips and said, "Close your eyes and come with me."

She did as she was instructed, and he took her hands to guide her across the room. Was it possible he was taking her to a locked box that held her ring? It was obvious her surprise was far from over. Maybe this was one of those proposals where the bride-to-be is sent on a treasure hunt. Now, that would be romantic!

With renewed optimism, Holly held on tight to Jared's hand as he led her toward the front wall of their apartment.

"Open your eyes," he finally announced.

Scanning the space around her, she searched for the next clue.

"Look," he instructed, "out the window."

Holly looked out and down. Next to her car was a second car, a compact one, with a bow on the top. She glanced back up.

"You bought me a car?" she asked, confused.

"Happy Birthday, baby!" he yelled again. "I told you I had something big and shiny planned! Now I won't have to borrow your car to get to work all the time. It's going to take so much pressure off of us."

"You bought this for you?"

"Well, it's for us, of course. You know. I figure we can switch off and stuff ... maybe every other week or something. What do you think? You're speechless, huh?"

"Yes, I think I am indeed speechless."

"I'm going to go get ready," Jared said. "I can't wait to drive this baby over to your parents' house."

"Wait," Holly said.

He turned around. "What's up, babe? You want to take it for a spin now? I guess that's okay."

"No, that's not it." She stared at him, trying hard to fight back her tears of disappointment.

"I really surprised you didn't I? Are you all right? You're acting kind of funny."

"No, Jared, I'm not *all right*," Holly responded.

"I don't get it, babe. In my book, this should be your best birthday ever. What's your deal?"

"My *deal* is I finally figured out we're reading two completely different books, and we always will be." She stared into his eyes and saw a blank expression looking back at her. He clearly did not understand any of her frustration. "I thought you were going to propose today. Ever since Ava's wedding, you've been saying stuff like you needed extra money to buy something special for me—for our future—something shiny. What the hell, Jared? *A car?* I thought you were talking about an engagement ring."

"I can't afford an engagement ring, babe, you know that. I got the car on the cheap from a buddy."

She looked at him and shook her head. "Jared, the ring is so not even relevant. Proposing is really just words ... from the heart. Last time I checked, that part didn't cost any money. Of course, you have to want to say the words. You have to have *the balls* to be able to say the words."

"This is bullshit. I bought you a freaking car, and this is the thanks I get? I'm going to take a shower."

"Yes, this *is* bullshit. You're right. You know what? I'm glad, too. Because now I know exactly how you really feel, and I can stop wasting my time. It's okay, though. You don't have to think about me anymore. I won't be here when you get out. In fact, after I move all my stuff, I won't be back again. Ever. Oh, and by the way," Holly said, grabbing the key to the new car before walking out the door, "thanks for the gift."

26

"Holly? Is that you?"

Ava came out of the kitchen with Jenna by her side, her face covered in chocolate.

"Aunt Holly!" she said, running into her arms.

"Hi, sweet pea! I sure did miss you!"

"Guess what? Grandma made five kinds of pie *and* cookies. I don't like pie, but I promised her I'd eat all of my beans, so she let me have a cookie before dinner. I took the chocolate one."

Holly looked at her niece's messy face. "You don't say," she laughed. "So did any of it wind up in your tummy?"

"Yup, and it was de-licious!"

Laughing, Ava tried to wipe her daughter clean with a napkin. "This little one already wore Mom out. She went upstairs to take a nap before dinner. The men are downstairs playing pool and watching the game. You know how they are." She gave her sister a hug. "It's so good to see you. Where's Jared?" She pulled back. "Are you okay?

Holly only shook her head, knowing the moment she said the words her tears would start flowing.

"Jenna, honey," Ava said, turning on the television, "why don't you take a little rest and watch TV until Grandma comes down. Mommy needs to talk to Aunt Holly for a little bit."

"Okay," her daughter replied, already distracted by the show in front of her.

Taking Holly's hand, Ava led her into the kitchen, where Tessa stood at the sink, washing dishes.

"Oh, hey, Holly. I didn't know you were here. Grab a towel. You can dry."

Holly sat at the kitchen table, burying her head in her hands.

"… or not," Tessa said, looking over to her sister before turning the faucet off. "What's going on?"

Ava put her arm around her sister.

"Jared gave me my birthday present today," Holly started, sobbing between her words. "He wanted to give it to me early. He was all excited about it."

"That's good right?" Tessa asked, bringing over the box of tissues that had been sitting on the counter.

"You told us he's been hinting at something *extra special* this year. Why are you crying?"

"It wasn't a ring."

"I know you're disappointed," Ava said, rubbing her sister's back, "but this doesn't mean it's not going to happen It just means it's not the right time."

Holly looked at her sister through her tears. "How much more time does he need?" She closed her eyes, letting all of the pent up anger, frustration, and sadness from years of waiting rush out of her body all at once. "I left him," she said, her body trembling as she spoke the words.

"Oh, sweetie," Ava said, turning her around to hug her. Tessa joined in as well.

"He bought me a car. Not a ring, a car. A used car. Not even for me, really, it was more for us to share … every other week. All this time—all the hints." Holly stopped to catch her breath, wiping her tears. "The point is there were no plans for making a commitment for a future together. The ring part wasn't even that important. He could have done so much with just words and actions to show me he cared about creating a bond that would last a lifetime. Instead, he gave me something that could break down at a moment's notice. It was a sign I needed to be done with him once and for all. He had no intention of proposing. I was a fool to think he'd changed."

Tessa sat down at the table with her sister and took her hands. "I'm really sorry, sis. Men suck."

"I know there's someone out there who's a thousand times better for you," Ava said, getting her sister a glass of water.

Taking a deep breath, she nodded. "The thing is, I feel like an idiot more than anything else. It took this for me to realize I wasn't in love with him, not even a little bit. I was in love with the *idea of him.* This fantasy I had in my head that I've had since I was a little girl—meeting the guy, getting married, having a family, living happily ever after. I was more in love with the idea that he could be the one to make it happen. I was so focused on my dream, I became blind to the person in front of me." She rolled her eyes. "Seriously? Jared?" She wiped her eyes again, and glanced up at her sisters. "I stayed with him for all of the wrong reasons. I know that now."

Ava sat down at the table, putting her arm around Holly. "Honey, you deserve so much better. And one day, you're going to find that person who's going to make all your dreams come true."

"Hol," Tessa began. "I ... um ..."

"What is it?" she asked with a concerned tone.

"Okay, promise you won't get mad. I only didn't say anything because you seemed so intent on this whole Jared thing. Well, it's about Ben."

"You two can be together now," Ava said, smiling. "You should talk to him. Mom invited him and his parents over today for Thanksgiving."

"Here? Today?" Holly sighed. She had thought about Ben her entire ride over. In fact, she hadn't been able to get Ben off her mind. "It's not going to happen. I saw him the other day, and he didn't seem happy to see me at all. Anyway, he'd only think I was interested because I didn't have Jared anymore. Today is going to be a disaster." She cradled her head in her arms, resting her elbows on the table.

"You need to know something," Tessa said, continuing where she left off. "Ben and I have been getting together."

"What?" Holly asked, lifting her eyes up. *So now the guy who she thinks her heart might actually belong to, is dating her sister?*

"No! Not like that. He'd kill me if I told you this, but, okay. At first it started as pool lessons. He asked Dad and me to teach him. He didn't want you to know. I guess he thought he could surprise you with a win. Don't worry, he's still really awful."

"You said *started as.* So it's something different now?" Sitting back up straight, she waited for her to explain.

"Yes, he's been texting me. He's got it bad for you, Hol. He's really a good guy. Here." She shoved her phone into Holly's hands.

She began to read the texts:

Ben: I can't stop thinking about her. I have to see her again.

Tessa: You can't. She's in a serious relationship. It's not fair to mess with her head like that.

Ben: I know. But, he's not the right guy for her. No, you're right. They seem to be doing better now. I need to let them be. Ugh. What is wrong with me?

Tessa: Do you want me to answer that?

Ben: No. I wish I could turn back time.

Tessa: Well then you'd still be that pimply boy wearing yellow ruffles.

Ben: You just made me snort coffee up my nose.

Tessa: That's what I'm here for.

Ben: Will you tell your sister I'm thinking about her?

Tessa: No.

Ben: Lol. Ok. But I am. Always.

Holly lifted her tear-streaked face and looked at her sister.

"This was from yesterday," Tessa said. "I think you should tell him you broke up with Jared."

Holly heard a cough and glanced over to see Ben standing in the doorway.

"How long were you standing there?" she demanded.

Grabbing another tissue, she wiped her face as best she could.

"I–I just got here," he said. "Max sent me in to get some drinks." He slowly walked into the kitchen toward the refrigerator, but stopped when he got to the table where Holly was sitting.

"We should go see how Jenna is doing," Ava said. Kissing Holly on the top of her head, she took Tessa's hand, and slipped out the kitchen door.

"Is it okay if I sit?" Ben asked.

She motioned to one of the empty chairs.

"You broke up with Jared?"

"There was really no point in me staying with him anymore. Our relationship wasn't going anywhere. It's for the best." Wiping her tears one more time, she tried to regain her composure. "I must be a mess."

"No," he said. "You look ... beautiful."

Peering at him through swollen eyes, she managed a smile. "You don't have to say that."

"I know."

"Thanksgiving is usually my favorite holiday," she said, picking up one of the cookies on the plate in front of her.

He paused before speaking, as if trying to think of just the right words to help her feel better. "It still can be, if you let it. It can only get better from here, right?"

"There's only one way to go from rock bottom and all that crap?" she asked, placing the cookie back down.

"I guess that did sound pretty cheesy."

"No, I appreciate it, thanks," she said.

He reached over to take her hand. "I know you probably need some time right now, but—"

"So, this is where you disappeared to. Geez, I ask you for a beer, and the next thing I know I have to send out a search party," Max said, walking in to the kitchen. He snatched two bottles out of the refrigerator.

Ben pulled his hand away and shoved a cookie into his mouth. "Sorry," he mumbled, "I got distracted by dessert."

Holly stood up to give her brother-in-law a hug.

"Oh hey, Hol, I didn't know you were here already. Listen, I've been sharpening my skills. I think I've got a chance of breaking your streak this time. You want to grab a beer and join us downstairs?"

"No," she said. "You guys go ahead. I wouldn't want to interrupt male bonding time, or whatever it is you fellows do with those sticks down there."

"Very funny," Max said. "After dinner then, and bring your A game, 'cause Miss Holly Haines is going *down.*"

"Yeah, yeah," she laughed, shooing him off. "That's what they all say."

"You're awfully quiet." Elbowing Ben, he shoved the beer into his hands. "Here."

He stood, following Max out of the kitchen, turning his head to gaze at Holly as he walked away.

27

Holly was quiet through most of dinner, giving short answers to the few questions asked of her, instead of the drawn out thoughtful responses her family had grown used to. Before they all sat down, she had pulled her parents aside to tell them about Jared. Her mother had been more upset than Holly thought she would be—she supposed she'd had her sights on a proposal for her middle daughter this year as well. Her father, on the other hand, appeared oddly relieved. Nobody mentioned his name during the meal. It was as if he never existed.

At first she tried her hardest during dinner not to make eye contact with Ben, but it wasn't easy. Her sisters had somehow managed to seat him directly across from her. It seemed every time she looked up she met his eyes—eyes, that no longer appeared lost, uncomfortable, or distant, but rather were warm, caring, and compassionate ... eyes that were accompanied by a smile that had so much to say. Feeling more at ease by the end of the meal, she found herself stealing glances and smiling back.

After desert, the men retreated to the basement, while the women finished cleaning up.

"Go to him," Tessa whispered, as they finished putting the last of the dishes away. "Trust me."

"I don't know," she responded. "Should I?"

"Oh for Heaven's sake," Ava said, grabbing her hand. "Come on, already." She pulled her out of the kitchen and into the living room, with Tessa at their heels.

"Ava, slow down!" Holly demanded, pulling her hand back.

They stopped just before they reached the basement steps.

"Enough games, Holly. The two of you were making googly eyes all through dinner. We all saw it. There's nothing holding either of you back anymore. I know it's only been a few hours for you, but you're a single woman now, *Ms. Haines.*"

"Go get him, tiger," Tessa added. Lifting her hands as if they were claws, she growled at her older sister.

"O-kay," Holly said, pushing her sister's hands back down. "Let's aim for some decorum here, shall we?"

"Oh, come on, loosen up a little," Tessa tousled Holly's hair.

"What are you doing?" she asked, smoothing it back down.

"Messy is in. Shake those blonde tresses out, like this." Her sister bent her head over and shook her long brown hair from side to side before whipping her head back.

Holly laughed. "You look like something out of a horror movie."

Tessa checked the mirror above the fireplace and straightened her hair a bit. "Okay, maybe not quite that much, but you look so ... I don't know ... school teacher-ish."

"I am a school teacher."

"Yeah during the day. But on your off hours, you need to get your sexy on."

"That's okay, thanks. Oh shit, they're coming up the stairs. Now what do I do?" Holly asked, hiding behind Ava.

"Um, you're going to talk to him," she said, stepping to the side.

Max came up the stairs first, carrying a sleepy Jenna, followed by Holly's dad, and Ed. Ben closed out the line.

"I think we need to put this little one to bed," Ava said, following Max up the stairs toward the guest room.

"Ed, how about that cigar I promised you?" Bob said as they all stood in the living room "Ben, are you interested?"

"No, thank you, sir."

"Suit yourself. Come on, Ed. Grab your coat. We have to go sit on the patio. If Patricia catches me smoking these things in the house, she'll kick me out for good."

"Okay ... well, I think I'm going to head back into the kitchen," Tessa said, scurrying off to leave Holly and Ben alone in the living room.

"Wow," Holly said, smiling at Ben. "I really know how to clear a room."

"I'm still here," he said.

"You are." Staring into his eyes, Holly was at a loss for words. She'd wanted this moment to happen, and yet, she didn't know what to do with it. She started to laugh quietly to herself.

"Am I that funny to look at?" he asked.

"No. I was thinking about how crazy this day wound up. I feel like I'm a completely different person than the one I was when I woke up this morning. Do you think it's possible for someone to grow that much in one day—not on a physical level, I mean—" She laughed again. "I'm sorry, I'm not making any sense, I know. I feel like my wants and needs have changed so dramatically in just a few hours. Has that ever happened to you?"

Taking her hands in his own, he gazed into her eyes. "Yes," he said, curling his lips back into a wide grin. "It happened the day you came to talk to me at Ava's wedding."

"There you are, Ben," his mother said, as she came into the room.

He let go of Holly's hands and turned around to greet her.

"I'm sorry to interrupt," she stated, not seeming to notice anything more than two friends who were talking, "but I feel a migraine coming on. Can you go find your father, and tell him I think it's time to go?"

"Of course, Mom," he said, helping her to a chair. "I'll be right back."

He smiled at Holly as he walked out of the room.

28

Holly spotted Ben as soon as she walked through the door of the restaurant. He rose to pull out her chair and took his own seat across from her.

"I'm sorry I couldn't get together with you yesterday," she said, "Ava and Max were only in town for a couple of days and my mom had a big Black Friday girls' day planned. It's hard having them so far away."

"You don't need to apologize." He gazed at her for a moment before continuing, "You look beautiful."

She smiled. "You know, you're going to have to stop telling me that every time you see me ... but, thank you."

"I speak only the truth," he said, grinning, "I could sit like this staring at you all night."

"I thought you said you weren't very good at talking with women? That sounded pretty smooth to me."

"I'm actually nervous as hell," he admitted sheepishly. "I'm terrified I'm going to do or say something to mess this up. I feel like I've been waiting for this from the moment we had our first kiss when we were sixteen."

"I don't think you have to worry. I kind of think you're cute. I have ever since you sat next to me in Freeman's history class. Do you remember?"

"Of course I remember," he said, with a twinkle in his eye. "I gave Bart Rivera an old Mickey Mantle baseball card that belonged to my father so I could have the seat next to you. I got in big trouble, but it was worth it."

"Really? I always wondered why he suddenly switched seats. I thought maybe I smelled or something."

"Nope. It was all my doing. Of course, after that I never said two words to you for the rest of the year, but still, I was just happy to be close to you. By the way, we don't bring that story up when we're around my dad, okay? Mantle's card is going for big bucks now, I hear." He cringed and shook his head.

"Got it," she said with a smile. "Wow, you're full of mysteries and secrets. You're like a box I can't wait to unwrap."

"Oh really now," he said, raising his eyebrows.

Putting her hands to her cheeks, she tried to hide her growing embarrassment. "That's not what I meant. Unravel is probably the better word."

"That works for me, too," he said, teasing her.

"Maybe we should change the subject—please? Is it time to order?" She checked around for the waiter. "I think I could use a glass of wine."

"I'm only playing—you don't have to be embarrassed. Although, you're really cute when you are. I have a weird sense of humor sometimes. Sorry."

As if on cue, the waiter appeared. Ben ordered a bottle of wine and asked for a few more minutes before ordering their food.

"I was thinking after dinner, we could go for a walk along the river. How does that sound to you?" he asked.

"I think that's a great idea," Holly said, wondering how he knew that was one of her favorite activities. It was one of those things Jared had always thought was a waste of time—probably because it didn't involve booze. "Before we know it, the path will be covered with snow. We might as well take advantage of the nice weather while we still have it."

The waiter returned with their wine and proceeded to fill their glasses.

"Thank you," she said and watched as he walked away.

"To first kisses," Ben said, clinking his glass against Holly's.

"And baseball cards," she added.

"I couldn't think of a more perfect second first date," Ben said as they strolled by the water, holding hands as they walked.

"Second first date?" Holly asked.

"Well, yes. Technically, our *first* first date was the Soph Hop."

"Wouldn't that make this our second date?"

"No," he said, curling his lips up. "Too much time has passed. The general rule of thumb is that a second date has to occur within a week—two weeks top. We've got a ten year lag here. Our clock reset ages ago."

Holly stopped walking. "You've put way too much thought into this," she said.

"Oh, you have no idea. You're pretty much all I've thought about since the wedding."

"Can I tell you something?" she asked. There was just enough light from the moon for her to see a shimmer in his eyes.

"Of course."

"I've had a hard time getting you off my mind as well," she confessed.

Leaning in close, she could feel his warm breath on her face. The reflection of the stars danced on the water behind them. "I've been dreaming of this moment," he told her, caressing her cheek lightly, his eyes peering deep into her, his stare going straight to her heart, as he moved even closer. "There's nothing keeping us apart anymore," he whispered.

"Nothing," she whispered back, feeling the softness of his lips touch hers.

29

"You don't think this is strange?" Holly asked, as she reached for the key her sister kept hidden above the doorframe before letting themselves in.

Ben placed the basket and blanket he'd been carrying on the floor and wrapped his arms around her waist, pulling her in.

"No," he said, alternating his kisses between her lips and her neck, sending shivers down her spine.

Releasing her slowly, he spread out the blanket on the floor of Tessa's studio apartment.

"She texted me this morning and said she'd be gone until midnight," he said.

Holly took a deep breath, still trying to regulate her heartbeat from the feel of Ben's lips on her. "That's what I mean. That she set this up with you."

Tessa had texted her as well. In addition to letting her know she'd be out late, Tessa also told her, rather crudely, which side of her bed squeaked the least. Holly wondered if she shared this information with Ben as well.

Ben sat on the blanket and began unloading the basket: several containers of food, wine, plates, glasses, and utensils—he'd thought of everything. She grabbed a couple of pillows off the couch and sat down next to him.

"It's not strange. She's sort of become my confidant I guess, at least where you're concerned. I had mentioned I wanted to take you on a picnic but it's too chilly, and she came up with this idea. I think it's romantic. She wouldn't have suggested it if it wasn't okay. I want to make you happy, that's all."

"You do, very."

Ben opened the bottle of wine, poured some into each of their glasses, and set them on the coffee table.

"First things, first." He took her hands. "You look beautiful, as always."

She shook her head and laughed. "There's that smooth talker again."

Staring at her with puppy dog eyes, he shrugged his shoulders. "One of these days you're going to believe me."

She reached over and took a sip of her wine, then leaned into his body as he dished out the rest of the meal.

"I wish every night could be like this," he said, placing a plate of chicken and pasta on the blanket in front of her.

Nodding, she felt happier and more content than she had in years. "Life doesn't get any better than this. How did we get so lucky?"

"It wasn't luck," Ben said, nuzzling her hair. "It was fate."

Holly turned around to look at him. "You *have* been talking to my sister a lot, haven't you? So, what else do the two of you talk about?"

"Well, now if I told you, she wouldn't be my confidant anymore, would she? But I'm curious as to why you're asking. Do *you* have secrets I need to unravel?" Looking at Holly with a mischievous grin he grabbed her around the waist, leaning her back. "Hmm, perhaps a good tickling will get them out of you."

"No, please," she begged, giggling. "No tickles. Anything but tickles."

"Anything?"

"No!" She slapped his hands away, still laughing. "But I do promise to share all my secrets."

"I suppose that will have to do for now. As long as you promise I can still do this." Leaning down, he found her parted lips, giving her a long sensual kiss.

"Yes," she whispered, trying to catch her breath, as she wrapped her arms around his neck, "I promise."

"Good morning, beautiful."

Holly pushed the covers aside, shivered when her bare feet touched the cold floor, and walked to her window. There was a fresh coat of snow on the ground. The first of the season. School would most likely have a delayed opening today while they cleared the roads.

"Good morning, yourself," she said into her phone.

By the time they finished their meal last night it was half past midnight. With no sign of her sister, Holly got up to check her phone.

Won't be home anytime soon. Lockup when you leave and don't forget ... stay to the left.

She shook her head and snickered. When Holly finally arrived back home thirty minutes later, her father was half-asleep waiting for her on the sofa with the excuse he hadn't realized what time it was and must have dozed off watching the news. Holly couldn't help but notice the television wasn't on. She smiled at him, gave him a kiss goodnight on the cheek, and walked up to her room, where she drifted off to sleep with visions of Ben's sparkling eyes gazing at her.

"I miss you already," he said. "When can I see you again?"

"Well ... how about tonight?" Holly asked, grinning.

Ben groaned. "I don't know if I can wait that long."

30

Holly zipped her dress and twisted around to see herself better in the mirror. She could still pass for a college student at almost twenty-six years old, even if she felt much older. At least *she* thought so.

"Is that what you're wearing?" Tessa asked, her tone making it sound like she'd been digging through the dumpster behind the local charity store.

"Um, no?" Sighing, Holly unzipped her dress and pulled it back over her head. "What should I wear? I don't exactly have a wardrobe for going to a nightclub."

Tessa flipped through the clothes in Holly's closet. "Bland, boring, basic... Seriously? This is all for work.

Where are your fun clothes? Didn't you keep any stuff from college?"

"You're looking at it. I wasn't really a nightclub kind of girl."

"Okay, fine," Tessa said, pulling out a purple blouse and black skirt. "Here, I suppose this will work, but try to hike the skirt up a little if you can, and maybe leave a few buttons on your shirt open."

"We're going to a nightclub, not a strip club," Holly said. "Besides, I'm meeting Ben there. I'd like to look nice, not trashy."

"He stopped texting me to cry over you, by the way. The last one I got was to thank me for letting you guys use my apartment. I guess that means things are going well?"

Holly smiled. It had only been a week since Thanksgiving, but she couldn't believe how happy Ben made her. They'd had a date every night since their river walk. Now that she was living at home again, it was a true courtship, something she never really had before. Ben came to her house, sat with her dad as he waited for her to finish getting ready, and dropped her off at the end of their date. It helped that her parents adored him.

"Yes," she said, "it's going great."

"And perhaps, that also means your little sister was correct about him and that whole fate thing?"

Holly rolled her eyes. "Yes, Tessa. You were right. We were meant to be together."

"Hold on" she said, grabbing her phone and pressing a button. She held it up to Holly's mouth. "Can you say that again, only try to enunciate a little more clearly this time."

"I *said*," she began. "I think it's time we got going. I told Ben we'd meet him there at nine." Crinkling her nose at Tessa, she walked out her bedroom door.

The club was dark and smoky—as most college haunts were—despite the laws that no longer allowed smoking inside these types of establishments. At least the floor in this place wasn't as sticky as the last one they'd gone to. Holly grabbed two beers and met her sister across the room at a small table.

"Is Ben here yet?" Tessa yelled over the music.

"I don't see him," she shouted back.

"So how's it going at Mom and Dad's?"

"It's weird being back at home, but I know it's only temporary. I'll start apartment hunting soon."

"Have you been in contact with Jared at all?"

"No. He's left a couple of messages and texts, but I'm not interested in the same old excuses. Now that he's got my old car, I've been able to tell when he's not home. I've been going over on my way home from school when he's not around to pick stuff up. I guess that gift actually wound up working out after all."

Holly laughed. "Anyway, I've got everything out now, so I have no need to go back. Last trip I made, I left the apartment keys on the coffee table."

"You should've tied them to his balls. Oh, yeah, he doesn't have any, I forgot."

"You have the mouth of a truck driver."

Tessa lifted her beer and clinked her sister's bottle.

"Hey, I thought that was you!" the familiar voice said, slapping Holly a little too sharply on the back.

She turned around in disbelief. "Dan? What are you doing here?"

"I know," he said. "I get that all the time. But even us principals like to loosen up and unwind every now and again." He did an odd hip thing and attempted to moon-dance backwards halfway across the dance floor, bumping into several groups of people.

"Is he drunk?" Tessa whispered loud enough for Holly to hear.

She shrugged, as he made his way back over doing the same bizarre dance step.

"So um," she began, "Tessa, this is Dan, the principal at my school. Dan, this is my sister, Tessa."

"Ah, another Haines sister. It's very nice to meet you. Are you also a math wizard?"

"Ew, no. I'm a theater major. Well, theater production, I mean."

"Oh, really? You should come to our talent show. It's going to be quite a performance ... especially the opening act. Isn't that right, Holly?" He elbowed her so hard, she nearly fell off her stool.

"Mmmm hmmm," she replied, straightening herself back up.

"Yes," Tessa said, laughing, "I've heard about this math rap the two of you are doing. Sounds ... intriguing."

"Well, your sister here is the mastermind behind it. I'm just along for the ride." Throwing his arm around Holly's shoulder, he leaned across the table to get closer to Tessa, flattening Holly's face into the tabletop, and added, "She's pretty amazing."

She tried to sit back up, but was stuck.

"So I've heard." Tessa continued to chuckle.

"Come on!" Dan yelled, pulling Holly back up and off her seat. "Let's go find Alex and show off some of our dance moves."

Yanking her off her chair, he swung her around, right into Ben's arms.

"Fancy meeting you here," he said, catching her.

"Thank you," she whispered as she gave him a kiss. "Ben, you remember Dan, don't you?"

"Yes, of course, nice to see you again."

Smiling wide, Dan punched Holly in the shoulder. "A kiss, huh? I see what's going on here." He winked. "When did this all start?"

"Dan, honey," Alex said, coming up from behind and holding on to his arm. "I think we need to get you some water." He looked over to Holly and Ben. "Believe it or not, this is from just one beer."

"Okay, sweet-ums," Dan said, tracing Alex's chest with his finger, "but then, I really want to dance."

Forty minutes later, and without any more alcohol in him, Dan seemed much more subdued, spending the entire time on the dance floor with Alex, Holly, and Ben, while Tessa, as usual, was holding court in the corner with a group of cute college boys.

"What a workout," Holly said as they headed back to their table.

"How about something cold to drink?" Ben asked.

"A beer would be great, thanks," she replied.

Within minutes, he returned with three bottles for Holly, Alex, and himself, and another glass of ice water for Dan.

"I can't remember the last time I had so much fun," Dan said, nodding his head along with the beat in the music. "Sorry if I was a little crazy earlier. I don't usually drink. I have zero tolerance in case you couldn't tell."

"I hadn't noticed," Holly said, trying not to laugh. "I thought you said you come here all the time?"

"No," he reminded her, "I said I like to unwind every now and again. That doesn't mean I go out drinking. It's actually my first time here. This was Alex's idea. What about you?"

"I've never been here before either. This is one of my sister's hangouts. Looks like tonight it's getting taken over by us old folks."

"Hey, who you calling old?" Alex asked. "I can go all night." Getting off his stool, he continued to dance, throwing his arms in the air while twisting his hips. He stopped suddenly and doubled over. "I just need to rest for a minute. I think I might have pulled something. I am getting old, aren't I? Shit."

Dan patted him on the shoulder. "It's okay darlin' we'll grow old together. We do need to go soon, though. It's a school night, you know."

Putting his arm around Holly's waist, Ben leaned into her. "I guess you can't call in sick tomorrow if you wake up too tired to go to work," he told her. "Your boss will know you're faking."

"That's right," Dan said, getting up. "The gig is up. See you bright and early, Ms. Haines."

"Yes, sir," Holly replied, nodding, trying her best to keep a serious face, yet failing horribly.

Dan put his hands on her shoulders and looked into her eyes. "I'm so glad to see you so happy. I hated how stressed and sad you were becoming before Thanksgiving." He turned to Ben. "It warms my heart to see the two of you together like this … beaming." He gave them both hugs. "Come on, Alex—we need to leave before I start bawling right here in the middle of this place." Hugging them again, he waved as he and Alex disappeared through the crowd.

31

66 **I** know it's only been a couple of weeks, but I can't help but feel like I've met my soul mate, Ava. For the first time, I can honestly understand how you felt when you came home from college and were talking about Max—gushing, really. The way your eyes lit up. I don't know—I've never felt this way before." Sitting at the desk in her bedroom, Holly looked at the doodled hearts she'd drawn on her memo pad back when she thought she and Ben weren't meant to be. That all seemed like a million years ago now.

"You can't see me smiling through the phone, but I am—an incredibly, huge, smile. Not just because I'm happy for you, but because I know Ben is such an amazing person. It runs in the family you know."

"Yeah, yeah. The other day I was thinking about everything. Remember how after I broke up with Jared, I had that whole realization that I was never in love with him, but I was in love with the *idea* of him?"

"I do. It was very profound."

"Well, that's the thing. With Ben, the only thing that matters to me is spending time with him. I couldn't care less if we get married. *He* is what's important to me. Not that he may or may not be a vehicle to fulfill this crazy dream of mine."

"You do see the irony there don't you?" her sister asked. "The fact that you just used the word vehicle to describe Jared ... you know, because he thought a car was what you wanted?"

"Oh, Ava," Holly said, shaking her head, laughing. "Only you would make that connection."

"I'm sorry. I couldn't resist. Anyway, I'm so happy for you. Do you two have any romantic plans for your birthday on Saturday?"

"He's taking me out for dinner. I was hoping we could spend the day together, but he'll be stuck in a training seminar for most of the day."

"I wish I could be there to celebrate with you. This living across the country is starting to get old."

"Is everything okay?" Holly asked.

"Yes, yes, it's fine. I guess I got a little spoiled being home so much this fall. I can't wait to see you again on Christmas."

"Me too. Take care of yourself, okay?"

"Promise. Love you."

"Love you, too."

32

"**H**appy Birthday, Ms. Haines!"

"What's this?" Holly walked into her classroom Friday morning to see all of her fifth grade students crammed together.

Dan stood by her desk with a huge box from Jake's Bakery. "Cupcakes!" he proudly announced.

"You didn't have to buy me cupcakes," she said to him, grinning. She was a bit embarrassed. He never made a big deal out of any of the other teacher's birthdays. No doubt she'd be the subject of staff lunchroom gossip today.

"I didn't," he said.

"Oh, well then." She laughed, feeling relieved. "Never mind."

"But they did." He pointed to her students. "And they made you cards. What can I say, Ms. Haines, your students adore you."

"Oh my! What a wonderful surprise!" She clapped her hands together, beaming. "Thank you all so much! I *do* have the best students." Holly looked at the stack of cards on her desk. "Should I open these now or wait until tomorrow when it's my actual birthday?"

"*Now!*" her class screamed out.

"Wow," Dan said, "and they haven't even had any sugar yet!"

"Speaking of, I suppose you're here because you want one of these, eh?" She motioned to the box of cupcakes with her head.

"Well, since you asked," he said. He opened the box, took out a cupcake, and shoved the entire thing in his mouth in one bite.

"*Hey!*" the kids all shouted, laughing.

Holly burst out giggling as well.

"Mr. Harper?" Elaine Fairview called out.

The entire room continued to laugh, not noticing Mrs. Fairview in the room.

"*Dan!*" she shouted at full blast.

Silence.

"Wef?" he mumbled, trying to chew and swallow at the same time without choking. He had green icing completely covering his lips and most of his chin. He looked like an overgrown toddler who was waiting for his mommy to wipe his mouth.

"A word please," Elaine said stoically.

Holly could swear she heard Dan groan. "Certainly, Mrs. Fairview. Enjoy the celebration, kids and happy birthday again, Ms. Haines." He grabbed a napkin off the desk and tried to clean up, but really all he did was smear the green frosting even further across his face.

"Thank you, Mr. Harper," Holly said, doing her best not to laugh as he left the room.

"You're in a good mood, Tessa said as she pulled up a couple of stools to the ledge in the back corner of Farrell's Pub. Holly hadn't been back since the night she and Jared went out with Ben and Michelle. That had been a disaster, although it had resulted in Ben and his *lovely* girlfriend breaking up, so that evening wasn't all bad. "I figured tonight would be one big sob fest. You know, *It's my birthday, and my boyfriend's out of town, wah, wah, wah.*"

Holly looked at her sister with a strange expression. "Uh, if I was thirteen maybe, but I'm not. Besides, my birthday is tomorrow."

"Trust me, I know," Tessa said. "I have to get up at the crack of dawn to come over. Apparently Mom's cooking you a big breakfast. I hope that wasn't a surprise."

Laughing, Holly took a sip of her beer. "No, it wasn't. And by crack of dawn, do you mean ten o'clock?" She smiled. "I'm the one picking you up. Breakfast is at ten-thirty."

"It *is* a Saturday." The corners of her mouth turned up, letting Holly know she was teasing.

"Well, I'm glad you're willing to give up your precious sleep to hang out with your big sis. It means a lot to me." Sitting up in her chair, she put her hands over Tessa's. "Family is so important," she said.

Her sister cocked her head. "You're not doing that weird meditation thing again, are you?"

"No! I'm just really happy. Do you know what I did today?" she asked.

"Taught math?"

"I didn't actually."

"But you're a math teacher."

"True, but today my students and I ate cupcakes and laughed, really laughed. We spent our math time getting silly. It was the most fun I've had in I don't know how long. Yes, we missed a day of math. Big deal. They wanted to help me celebrate my birthday, and that's what we did. It taught me to appreciate the good and throw out the bad."

"So you're admitting math is bad," Tessa noted.

"You're missing the point."

"I'm just playing with you. That one was too easy," she said, smiling.

"Today taught me to appreciate everything around me. My job, Ben, my awesome students—"

"Don't forget about your extraordinary family. They really should have been at the top of your list you know, especially one sister in particular. The cute one with the name that starts with a T."

"Yes, and I'm extremely grateful for my extra special family, my sister Tessa in particular," Holly told her.

"Cheers to that," Tessa said, holding up her bottle. "And happy early birthday."

33

"What's all this?" Holly asked.

Ben picked her up for her romantic birthday dinner at six o'clock as promised, but instead of taking her to a restaurant, he took her back to his apartment. It smelled wonderful—as good as any five-star establishment.

"I'm cooking for you," he said. "I'll bet you didn't know I had mad culinary skills. It's one of those mysteries about me you still have yet to unwrap ... or was it unravel?

He kissed her lips and neck as she tried to take off her coat. Slipping it off and onto the floor, she wrapped her arms around his back, pulling him in tighter. She could skip dinner entirely and kiss him all night long. She wanted to do other things to him as well, but they agreed to take things slow, at least where that was concerned. Holly had jumped right into bed with Jared and moved in with him too soon. As much as she was sexually attracted to Ben, she told him right from the start she wanted an old-fashioned romance this time around. Standing there in his arms, feeling the passion rise in her body, she was wondering if she made the wrong decision. She reluctantly, pushed him away.

"Whoa," was all she could manage to say as she tried to collect herself.

"Whoa," he repeated, obviously flustered as well. "Okay, so I'm going to go get dinner together and perhaps take a cold shower."

Holly giggled as she followed him into his kitchen. "So Chef Ben, what's on the menu this evening?"

Opening his oven, he pulled out a baking dish. "Chicken Marsala," he proudly announced.

"It looks and smells fabulous," she said. "Let me get some—" As she walked toward the cabinets, something shiny in the trash bin caught her eye. *Were those empty take-out containers?* She grabbed two plates and turned back to the stove.

"So, Ben," she began, placing the dishes on the counter next to him, "I've always wanted to learn how to make Chicken Marsala. What type of wine do you use?"

"Oh, you know," he said, reaching for a serving spoon. "Any type of wine works, but I like a good quality wine. For this dish I used a ..."

She saw him glance at the unopened bottle by the sink.

"... Merlot."

"Really?" she asked. "Wouldn't you use, oh, I don't know, a *Marsala?*" She put her hand up to her mouth to hold in her laughter.

"Ok, you got me," he said, chuckling along with her. "I didn't actually make this. But I can cook—just nothing this fancy."

"I think it's sweet," Holly said, wrapping her arms around his waist. "But next time you need to do a better job of hiding the evidence. You *almost* got away with it." She nodded toward the trash.

"Wow," he said, shaking his head, "I was so close. Hey, did you know I'm a master pastry chef, too? Just wait until you see what I made you for desert."

Holly laughed. "I'm sure I'll love it."

"Everything was wonderful, thank you," Holly said, as she finished the slice of the birthday cake Ben *made* for her.

"The flowers!" Jumping up, he raced into his bedroom, returning with a bouquet of roses and daisies already in a vase that had a big red bow around them. "I'm making a mess of this evening," he said, shaking his head. "These are for you."

"They're gorgeous, thank you."

Placing them on the table, she pulled out the card.

For my beautiful Holly-

Our first kiss at sixteen, and now we celebrate your twenty-sixth birthday.

Ten years later, my life is finally complete.

xoxo - Ben

Sitting at the table, she stared at the man across from her. She couldn't believe what a dramatic turn her life had taken in such a short period of time. A tear escaped the corner of her eye.

"Why are you crying?" Ben asked. "Did I do something wrong?" Getting out of his seat, he rushed around the table and knelt down beside her.

"No," she said, wiping it away. "I'm just so … happy. So truly happy."

Ben cupped her face and kissed her as her tears continued to fall. "I am, too," he said, smiling. "More than I've ever been."

"I'm sorry. I don't know why I'm reacting like this." She pulled away slightly to meet his eyes. She could see it in the way he gazed at her, the way he kissed her, the way he held her. "I think it's because I'm—"

"—in love," he said, finishing her sentence. "I'm in love with you, Holly. I have been for a while now."

"Yes," she said, smiling a wobbly smile, "I'm in love with you, too." Holly savored every taste and sensation of Ben's lips as they kissed again, promising herself she would remember this moment forever.

34

"What are you doing here?" Holly asked, surprised to see Ben as she opened the door. It was a rare quiet Saturday morning with her parents out doing some holiday shopping. She had decided to take advantage of the time to catch up on grading papers.

"Oh, I was in the neighborhood, you know just driving around on this lovely morning" he said, with a mischievous expression on his face. "Can't a fellow stop in to say hello to his love every now and again?" He reached across the doorway and kissed her. "Well, aren't you going to let me in?"

"Sure," she said, matching his grin, "come in." She tilted her head and narrowed her eyes. "You're up to something, though. What is it?"

"Oh, Holly, so suspicious, you are. I already told you. I was in the neighborhood ... and I happened to notice your folks' car wasn't in the driveway."

"Ah," she said, nodding. "Now I see your motivation. Feeling frisky are we?"

"Who me?" he asked, pointing to himself. Hugging Holly tightly, he nipped at her earlobes. "You know I'm a perfect gentleman."

"And how do you know *both* my parents aren't home? It *is* possible my mom is still here. She could walk in on us at any second you know."

"She could," he agreed, moving on to her lips, "except I just saw them over at the diner finishing up breakfast." He pulled back and smiled. "They told me they were headed to the mall." He peered up at the ceiling as if deep in thought. "Going to the mall a week before Christmas—I'd say they're going to be gone all day, don't you think?" He raised his eyebrows and went back giving her playful kisses on her lips.

"It's possible," Holly said, looking out the window at her father's car pulling up the driveway. "Or knowing my dad, he'll get frustrated he can't find a parking space, turn around, and come home." She motioned to her parents walking toward the door.

Groaning, Ben let go of Holly as they entered.

"Ben, hello," Patricia said as they walked in. "Twice in one day, well, this is a treat."

"Nice to see you again, too."

"Damn traffic," Bob grumbled as he shut the door behind him.

"Tough morning, Dad?"

He shook his head. "Next time I get *that* brilliant idea, somebody please knock some sense into me. He settled into his chair and picked up the newspaper."

Holly looked at Ben. With her Dad now sitting in the living room, they didn't have many options.

"Are you up for a game of pool?" Ben asked.

Holly grinned. "Sure. I heard you've been getting lessons on the side. Let's see what you've got."

Taking Ben's hand, she led him down the basement steps. As soon as they reached the table, he grabbed her, resuming where he left off upstairs.

"I thought you said you wanted to shoot pool," Holly said, twisting around to place the triangle on the table. She tried to pull away from Ben long enough to set up the balls, but he wouldn't let go of her waist.

"I do," he said, kissing the back of her neck.

She sighed, letting go of the balls in surrender as he turned her toward him. He gently pushed her against the wall, his tongue tracing the edge of her lips before bringing his lips down on hers. She ran her hands across the breadth of his shoulders, and up to his cheeks, feeling his stubble along the tips of her fingers.

Pulling back slowly, he whispered, "Okay, I'm ready."

"Ready?" she asked, trying to catch her breath.

"Yes," he responded with a sexy smile. "To play pool."

She tilted her head. "So you think by kissing me you're going to throw my game off?"

"Well, to be honest, those lessons your dad and sister gave me didn't help a whole lot, so this is my plan B."

"I see," Holly said, biting her lower lip. She grabbed the triangle and finished setting up. "Do you want to go first?"

"Sure, why not?"

He grabbed a stick from the rack on the wall and lined up the cue ball. Holly watched as he brought it back and slid it forward with a good amount of force. While he managed to hit the cue ball this time, he somehow missed all fifteen balls that were set up perfectly in the center.

"Um, Ben? Just curious—What happens if plan B doesn't work?" she asked with a twinkle in her eye."

Ben laid his stick down, raised his eyebrows, and put two hands flat on the table. "Well, Ms. Holly Haines, then we move on to plan C."

He moved to his left and chased her in a playful manner as she shrieked, "Benjamin Oakes! Don't you dare!"

In a swift, single move, he lifted her up, one arm around the back of her waist, and the other under her knees. Lowering her down onto the section of the table that was ball-free, he gazed into her eyes. "Did you just dare me?"

She threw her arms around his neck as he leaned down to kiss her once again.

35

"What time is Ben coming?" Patricia asked as they finished cleaning the dishes from their Christmas dinner.

"He texted me about twenty minutes ago. His family is still eating. His parents apologize again they can't make it, but they always go to his mom's sister's house. Ben said he's going to try to sneak out early, but he's not sure he'll make it in time for dessert."

"Come on now, we all know he's not coming for dessert anyway," Tessa said, winking. "Well, he is, but not the kind Mom's putting out."

"Tessa!" her mother reprimanded. "That's enough out of you. Honestly! I don't know where that mouth came from."

"What? I didn't say anything wrong. I'm just talking about dessert." She smiled and winked at Holly again.

"It's a good thing Jenna is upstairs playing with her dolls," Ava said shaking her head.

"Speaking of," Patricia said, "I'm going to go upstairs to see my little grandbaby. Call me when you're all ready for pie."

"Okay, Mom," Ava said. "No rush."

"Hey, Holly," Tessa said, taking a seat on the couch, "Why don't you show Ava and me the math rap you're working on. I'm dying to see it."

"Sorry. You're going to have to wait two weeks like everyone else."

"That's not fair! Alex gets to see it, and he's not even related to you," Tessa said, pouting.

"Yeah, but he's our stage manager."

"Um, excuse me? I think I need to see his credentials. I'm the one with the theater background, remember?"

"And what about me?" Ava asked. "I won't be here in two weeks. I'll be back in California."

Holly sighed. "You two and your peer pressure. But I can't. It's a duet, and my partner isn't here." She shrugged her shoulders and smirked. "Sorry."

Tessa leaned over to Ava. "Don't worry, you'll get to see it when I post it on YouTube."

"I swear, if you—" A knock on the door interrupted her sentence. "I'll get it."

She swung the door open expecting it to be a few of the neighbors caroling.

"Ben?" she asked in surprise. "That was fast. I thought you were still eating."

"I need to talk to you." He looked over at Ava and Tessa sitting on the couch. "Alone if you don't mind."

"Let's go see what the guys are doing downstairs, shall we?" Ava asked, heading to the steps.

"Uh, sure," Tessa said, following her sister. She stopped to glance back at Holly before going down. "Holler if you need us, okay?"

"Yeah," Holly said, feeling a knot forming in the pit of her stomach. "Ben, what's the matter?"

"Can we sit?" he asked.

Holly nodded. "You're scaring me," she said as she sat down next to him.

He took her hands in his own. "I'm sorry. I don't mean to. I just — After I texted you, I got a phone call." He looked down and pulled his hands away to run them through his hair.

Turning his head toward her, she could see he'd been crying. "From who? Is someone sick? Ben, please. Talk to me." She slid closer to him and rested her head on his shoulder.

"It was from Michelle. I don't know how to tell you this."

"Michelle?" she asked, sitting back up. "Tell me what?"

Taking a deep breath, he let it out slowly. "She called me to tell me she's pregnant ... with my child."

Holly shut her eyes, feeling her body shut down piece by piece. First her mind, then her lungs, and finally her heart, as it shattered into a million pieces. "I need air," she whispered, running outside.

"Holly, wait!"

The bitter cold stung her skin as she crouched onto the front lawn, her tears almost icicles.

"Holly," Ben said, wrapping his coat and arms around her. "Please, come back inside, it's freezing out here."

She let him take her hand and guide her back into the house. Keeping his coat wrapped around her, she sat back down on the couch, paralyzed by her thoughts.

"Hol, this doesn't change anything between us. You are the one I love. Only you. I can help raise the baby without being a part of Michelle's life."

She willed herself to speak. She needed to get the words out, regardless of the pain they would inflict upon her soul. Unable to look him in the eyes, she spoke in a voice filled with despair.

"No, this changes everything. You have a child to think about. You have to at least give it a try with

Michelle. I could never forgive myself if you didn't. Family means everything."

"Holly, don't do this…"

She stood up tall on shaky legs and handed Ben his coat. "I think you should leave now."

36

"**H**ello?"

"Hey, hey … It's New Year's Eve! Who's the party girl? It's Holly! Woot!" Alex and Dan screamed together into the phone. Holly pulled the phone about a foot away from her ear so as not to result in any permanent hearing loss.

"Um? OK?" she said, laughing.

"It was a rap. Couldn't you tell?" Dan asked.

"I told him it sounded more like a cheer," Alex chimed in, "but he didn't believe me."

"No, it was great," she said. "Sort of like a chap or a reer. I loved it." Judging by the background sounds of the television, they were on speakerphone in their family room.

"Oh, you know, we're just trying to cheer you up. So, what's the plan for tonight?" Dan asked. "Something spectacular I hope?"

"Well, nothing big really. I told Tessa I might meet her out later for a drink, but I'll probably pass. She's going to a bar that's having one of those huge New Year's Eve dance party things. It's going to be crazy. I'm not in the mood for that."

Holly sat down on her bed. She missed the New Year's Eve days when she was younger, and she and her sisters would all sit around the television in their pj's watching the ball drop. Now with Ava back in California, Tessa preferring to hang out at parties, and Ben back with Michelle, Holly didn't know where she fit in.

"I guess I'll work on lesson plans while I watch the ball drop with my parents."

"Nonsense!" Dan squawked. "As your boss, I'm telling you there will be no work tonight. That's an order. And as your friend, I'm telling you we'll be by in an hour to pick you up. Make yourself pretty, Ms. Holly Haines, we're taking you out for a nice dinner, and after we'll go back to our place to ring in the new year in style."

"And by style," Alex interjected, "he means falling asleep with nachos hanging out of his mouth ten minutes before midnight."

"I've only done that twice," Dan said.

"But—"

"No buts! Don't make me start rapping again, because I'll do it."

"Oh, he will," Alex said, sounding terrified. "Please, Holly, I'm begging you. For the good of all mankind, do what he says!"

"Nah," she teased. "I don't believe him. He doesn't have it in him."

"What?" Dan retorted. "You know I will. First thing Monday morning when we're back from winter break, I'll rap all about how Holly Haines sat home all alone on New Year's Eve … over the intercom."

"Hah! That sounds like a nursery rhyme gone bad or something," Alex told them. "You don't want him to do that. It could get ugly and scare the kids."

"Then," her boss continued, "I'll send Gus Shaw and Elaine Fairview down to your room. I'll tell Mrs. Fairview you're the one who came up with the idea of adding an extra math section to each grade. She'll never leave you alone. Finally, I'll tell Gus you think all of the math teachers should wear a standard uniform, and that he should be the guy to design and make them. Before you know it, you'll be a human calculator. Kids will be coming up to you, poking you all day long."

"Ew, that's obscene, Dan," Alex said. "I kind of like it."

"Oh, get your mind out of the gutter, Alex," he said. "That's not where the buttons would go! I'm talking about kids here."

"No, please! Stop! I'll go. Just.stop.now.please." Holly was laughing so hard she could hardly catch her breath.

"Ah, I had a feeling you'd see things my way. See, Alex? I knew I could persuade her."

"You are good," he agreed.

"So, see you in an hour, then? And wear that little floral dress you have. It's really cute."

"Good-bye, guys," she said, still chuckling.

Holly hung up the phone and smiled. Her life might be falling apart, but she could always count on Dan and Alex to cheer her up. She pulled the floral dress out of her closet and held it up against her body, staring at her reflection in the mirror. Yes, the floral dress was definitely the way to go.

Dan and Alex made reservations at the Woodland House even before Holly agreed to go out with them. They picked the restaurant, knowing she would want something low-key, charming, and out of the main thoroughfare of partiers. They were right. It was the perfect place for them to have a relaxing dinner. They were good friends. The best she'd ever had, outside of her sisters, of course.

"Now, isn't this better than worrying about ex-boyfriends and lesson plans?" Dan asked, digging in to the apple pie he ordered.

"Much," Holly agreed. "Thank you." She scanned the restaurant. "I'm surprised this place isn't more crowded for a major holiday."

"Oh, it will be," Alex said. "Their New Year's festivities haven't kicked in yet. They've got the fancy five-course *prix fixe* menu like everyone else," he stated in his best snooty tone. "I wanted to eat normal food, so we came before that began."

"That's code for we're cheap," Dan chimed in. "I promised the maître d' we'd free up his table before eight. We'd better hurry up before they boot us out."

"Nonsense," Alex said. "I'll stay until I'm good and ready to leave."

The waiter walked by and placed the check on the table without asking if they'd like to order anything else.

"Um, I think they're trying to tell us it's time," Holly said, laughing.

"Oh, fine," Alex said, shoveling in the last bite of his dessert.

She reached down for her purse, but Dan grabbed her hand.

"No you don't. This one's on us. We never did get to take you out for your birthday."

"You guys are too good to me," she said, smiling. "I'm going to go use the ladies room. I'll be right back."

Pushing her chair back to stand up, she accidentally knocked into someone. "I'm so sorr—"

"Ugh," the shrill voice began. "Look what you've— You! You've spilled my drink all over my dress."

Holly couldn't help but stare at her protruding belly. "Michelle," she said, taking a napkin off the table and handing it to her. "I didn't see you there. I'm sorry." Looking around, she wondered if Ben was with her.

"Madame," the waiter said, rushing to her side, to take her glass, "Please, let me get you another Perrier."

Through the distance she saw him approaching. "Sorry about that," he said as he made his way up to her, "there was a line at the coat room. Oh."

Dan and Alex immediately stood up, apparently realizing who this woman was now that they saw her with Ben.

"Holly, we should go," Dan said. He threw a bunch of bills on the table and gently took her arm.

"Yes," she said, unable to take her eyes off of him. "O-okay."

The tears started before she reached the exit.

37

"Are you sure you're doing okay?" Ava asked.

Holly adjusted the gold chain around her neck. She promised Dan she would be back at school no later than a quarter to seven as they were due to go on stage at seven o'clock. He wanted her there earlier, but she needed a break from him. In an effort to keep her mind off Ben, he and Alex had her in rehearsals nearly every waking moment she wasn't teaching. It was exhausting, although she did appreciate the sentiment. Dan meant well, and for that she loved him. She loved both of them.

"No, but I suppose I will be. I don't really have a choice. I look ridiculous by the way," she laughed under her breath while staring at herself in the mirror.

She wore black nylon track pants, which had white stripes going down the sides of the legs, and a matching black T-shirt with an iron-on decal across the front that read: Don't be a Fool, Math is Cool. Topping off the ensemble were the accessories: gaudy fake gold chains as well as sweatbands on her head and wrists. Dan would be wearing the exact same outfit. The attire was Alex's idea. Holly felt completely absurd. She looked like ... she wasn't quite sure what ... some sort of a rejected athlete wanna-be from the eighties or something. She certainly didn't look like a hipster rapper. Of course, it was still better than the giant puffed out addition and multiplication sign costumes Gus had proposed.

"Text me a picture," Ava insisted.

"Um, no. Anyway, I have to run. Wish me luck. But no leg breaking, please. I have enough problems."

"Good luck. I'll be watching for you on YouTube later."

Holly snickered before hanging up. Her comment wasn't even worth a response.

"You made it!" Dan said with a sigh of relief.

"Of course I did," she said. "Did you think I'd bail?"

"He only wakes up in sweats every night with that same re-occurring nightmare," Alex replied. "You two look awesome, by the way."

"Thanks, I think."

"Anyway, everything's all set. Say the word, and I'll dim the lights and lift the curtain. It's just about seven o'clock."

Dan looked like a nervous wreck. "Shall we?" he asked, holding out his hand.

Nodding at Alex, she eagerly took her bosses hand and gave him a reassuring smile. "We've got this."

Gus walked out onto the middle of the stage in the gymnasium, which also doubled as an auditorium when the need arose, as Holly and Dan stood in the wings. He was dressed like a jester. It was her boss' idea to give him the role of Master of Ceremonies for the evening, thus ensuring he didn't actually perform. At least, she hoped he wasn't going to perform. Looking at his getup she wasn't so sure.

"Ladies and gents and children of all ages," Gus began as everyone took their seats.

Holly peeked out from behind the curtain. It was a packed house. There were even some people standing along the back wall. She saw Tessa sitting in the third row and waved. Her sister waved back, holding up her smart phone. If she dared take a video of her performance, Holly would kill her.

"We've got a great night planned for you and even some unexpected surprises," Gus rambled on.

Uh-oh. Surprises from Gus were never a good thing. Maybe he *was* planning something. Judging by the look on Dan's face, he was thinking the same thing.

"Your children have been working very hard on their routines, and I can tell you from watching rehearsals this afternoon, you're about to see some things that will leave you … um, speechless … in a good way, you know. It's all good. The children are fabulous, of course. As are the adults. Speaking of, let's get this show started with two of our favorite adults: Ms. Haines and Mr. Harper!"

Dan led Holly to the middle of the stage as the music started in the background. Well, not really music, it was more of a rhythmic beat for them to follow along to. They began moving their arms and legs to the sound perfectly in sync, just as they practiced.

Holly started first. "How are we all doing tonight?" she shouted.

The crowd cheered.

"Come on! I know you can be louder than that! Let's all make some *noise*!" Dan yelled.

The crowd screamed even louder.

She counted beats in her head as the cheers died down: *five, six, seven, eight.* She began the rap, "Yo, yo, let's get on the floor, 'cause I want to tell y'all a story 'bout the number four. You see four alone is pretty great, but add two of them together to get the number eight."

Dan looked at Holly and shook his head. "Eight?" he shouted out. "I can do better than that. Listen here." He waited for the beat to return to the beginning and then picked up the rap, "The number three has a funky groove, multiply them together and watch them move. Three times three makes the number nine, just remember that, and you'll be fine."

Holly pushed Dan gently to the side and yelled, "Nine was so yesterday!" The crowd cheered even louder.

He pretended to brush dust off his pants before getting back in line next to her. He resumed his dance steps in perfect sync once again. "Oh yeah?" he asked.

"Yeah," she replied, nodding and smiling.

He shook his head and turned to the crowd. "How about this?" He returned to his rap voice. "One, two, and seven are numbers called primes, I'd like to see you work them into your little rhyme."

Holly shooed Dan away with her hand. "No problem," she spoke, and then started rapping again, "Prime numbers are a handy tool, they need no other numbers to make them cool." She smirked as she prodded the audience to cheer her on. They were more than happy to oblige.

Dan hung his head and laughed. "Okay, okay," he said, still moving his arms and feet to the beat. "You win."

She smiled. "Not yet!" she yelled and counted the beat in her head. "You see the best kept secret is the number five, it's crisp and clean, and that's no jive. Anytime you want to multiply, it ends in itself or a zero and that's no lie."

"True story," Dan agreed, shrugging, while keeping his hands moving.

Holly glanced at him and giggled. As she moved her head to scan the audience, she noticed a face toward the back of the room. *Ben?* She missed the beat to the next line, and Dan gently nudged her. She looked at her boss and then back at the seat where she thought Ben had been sitting. The seat was empty. She kept moving her feet in rhythm, waiting for the starting beat to come back around, and nodded to Dan that she was ready.

They rapped together, "But our favorite number is the number ten, put your hands together, and let's do it again. Ten-nine-eight-seven-six-five-four-three-two-one! Math rules!"

They clasped hands, brought them up high and took a long deep bow as the crowd cheered. They came back up, waved to the audience, and ran off the stage.

"Oh my God, that was so much fun!" Holly shrieked, hugging Dan. "Sorry about the little snafu there. I lost my place for a second."

"I don't think anyone noticed," Alex said, coming out from the wings. "You two took the house down. That was great!"

"It was all Holly!" Dan told her, beaming.

"No, it was definitely a group effort," she said, looking around.

"Either way, it was fabulous," Alex said. "I gotta go help set up for the next act, a piano solo." He put his finger in his throat like he was trying to gag himself.

He walked over to the piano, getting ready to wheel it on stage, while Dan moved back to the sidelines to watch as Gus introduced the next act.

Tessa came running backstage, nearly knocking Holly over. "That was awesome! If you were my teacher, I so would have loved math."

"Well, it's never too late to start," Holly joked. "I have an extra seat in my classroom."

"Um, I'll pass, thanks."

"Listen," she said. "You didn't see Ben here, did you?"

"Ben? No, why would he be here?"

"No reason," she said, feeling her euphoria going down a bit. "It must have been someone else. Forget I asked."

"**A** new outfit will cheer you up," Tessa said while rummaging through racks of clothes.

"I don't need to be cheered up," Holly told her. "I'm fine."

With the talent show now over, Holly felt like her life was on auto-pilot. She got up in the morning, went to work, sat through the occasional staff meeting, and came home where she usually spent her evenings having dinner with her parents, grading papers, and working on lesson plans. Socially she hung out with either Tessa or Dan and Alex. Life was ... okay. She missed Ava, and she missed ... "*Ben?*"

"Where?" her sister asked.

"Over there," Holly said, motioning outside of the store to the area of the mall where there were benches. He sat facing them with his head down while he typed on his phone.

"You know he's back to texting me almost every day. You should go say hello."

"What's the point?" Holly asked, sadness in her voice as she peeked at him from behind the racks. "I'm trying to forget about him, remember?"

"He's miserable. He may be even more miserable than you are. At least you don't have to deal with Michelle on a regular basis."

"True," she noted. "But I don't think talking to him is a good idea."

"Okay, sis," Tessa said, buried under a pile of clothes she was trying to balance without toppling over. "I'm going to go try these on."

Continuing to spy on him, Holly moved up one rack at a time, as if on a covert mission, until she was close to the door at the opening of the mall. As she prepared to move up to the final rack, the one that would bring her closest to the bench where he was sitting while still allowing her to remain hidden, he lifted his head and met her eyes. She had no choice but to stand tall and walk through the front entrance of the store, as if that were her intention the entire time. She wished her heart would stop pounding so loudly.

He stood to greet her. "What are you doing here?" he asked.

Play it cool, Holly. She looked around at all the stores and raised her eyebrows. "Uh—shopping?"

"Right," he said shaking his head. "Sorry, I'm a little nervous right now. You tend to do that to me." The corners of his lips turned up showing her the sexy smile she'd missed so much. "How've you been?"

Horrible. Heartbroken. Distraught. Devastated. "Okay, I guess. How about you?"

He shrugged. "I saw you a couple of weeks ago, on stage. You were really good."

"That *was* you. I thought so. What were you doing there?"

"I needed to see you again." He looked down at the floor. "I'm sorry, I know I shouldn't have..." His phone began to ring.

He groaned and pulled it out of his pocket.

"Hello?"

"I'm done. Meet me at the entrance of Nordstrom's."

The phone wasn't on speaker, but Holly could hear the words clear as day. She'd recognized that shrill demand anywhere. Michelle hadn't even waited for his response before she hung up. Holly's heart sank.

"Her Majesty awaits," she said with a forced grin.

Appearing somber, Ben reached for her hand. "I don't want to leave you, but if I don't go she'll come looking for me."

Closing her eyes for a second, she pulled her hand away. "It's okay. I have to get going anyway."

She ran off before he could see her tears, finding Tessa as she was coming out of the fitting room.

"What's the matter? Why are you crying? Did you talk to him?"

Wiping her eyes, she nodded. "It's just—everything. Every time I see him, I feel such a strong pull … in my heart. It's so unfair."

Tessa dropped the clothes onto the top of the nearest rack and wrapped her arms around her sister, holding her close.

39

"Valentine's Day was surely a holiday created by some sadistic person hoping to torture all of the single people in the world," Holly said, filling her glass with wine.

They sat in Tessa's tiny apartment, wallowing over the fact it was February fourteenth and neither one of them had a significant other.

"Actually," Tessa stated, pouring a glass for herself, "I have visions of this big roundtable, with a bunch of guys sitting around it somewhere in the 1800s or something, and having a conversation like this ..."

"Aye, Arthur, we need to make more money this year. Our garden productions were fine, but the demand was just not what it should have been."

"Indeed, Theodore, my printing business has been on the decline as well. How has your confectionary business been, Herbert?"

"I declare, they've been frightfully low. If only we could think of a way to increase the demand for chocolate."

"And flowers," added Theodore.

"And cards," Arthur stated. "Even if it were for just one day a year, it would help. Perhaps Edward could even benefit with jewelry sales as well."

Holly smirked and finished her glass. "The dirty bastards. Look what they've created." She sat back on her sister's couch and stared out the window.

"Oh, don't let it get to you. It's only a stupid holiday."

"Do you think I made a mistake?" she asked. "Breaking up with Jared, I mean? It's just … Ben is with Michelle now and starting a family, and Jared *was* trying. Maybe I was being too impatient."

"Holly!" Tessa said sternly. "Do you need me to make a list of all the reasons why breaking up with Jared was the absolute *best* thing for you to do? I know you're upset about Ben, but that doesn't mean you have to settle. What about your whole you never loved him, you only loved the idea *of him*? There are plenty of guys out there—guys who will treat you the way you deserve to be treated. Listen, any other day, you'd totally agree with me. In fact, I'm pretty sure you've given *me* this speech before. The only reason you're saying any of this is because it's Valentine's Day, and you're getting caught up in all this romantic couples stuff. Take today to celebrate *you!* You can still make Arthur, Theodore, Herbert, and Edward happy."

"Who?" she asked confused.

"You know, my 1800s guys from my roundtable discussion. You should go buy yourself some chocolates and flowers. Not a card though—that would be kind of weird—sorry, Arthur. But you definitely deserve a nice piece of jewelry. Who says you're not allowed to pamper yourself?"

"Is that what you did today?" Holly asked.

"Me? No, I'm just a starving college student, but you're a teacher with a salary. Who, I might add, is mooching off Mom and Dad for the moment, so I gather you've got some bucks in your wallet."

"I'm not mooching, I'm saving so I can afford a decent place to live. There's a difference. All the places I've checked out so far are so expensive ... I wonder what he's doing today.

"Who, Jared?"

"No, Ben."

"Oh, that's easy," Tessa replied. "He's getting dragged to an over-priced restaurant where Michelle will order her expensive imported bottled water and a salad that will probably consist of a leaf of lettuce and half a cherry tomato. But it will look fabulous because the raspberry vinaigrette will be artfully splattered across the plate to look like one of Picasso's works of art. However, she won't eat it. Instead, she'll complain that she actually wanted the Van Gogh. The entire meal will cost as much as you make in a week. Trust me, Ben's even more miserable than you are."

"And that's supposed to make me feel better? Why are you so upbeat? Didn't some guy dump you the other day? I was expecting you to be as depressed as I am, but instead you're like the head of the pep rally. It's kind of annoying."

"Well, excuse me. Sorry to crash your pity party. I am in a good mood, actually. Not only was that guy I dated a douche, but I found out he moved on to Marney Springer. Last I heard, she has crabs. I expect his Valentine's Day will be a little ... um ... itchy." She danced around like she had ants in her pants, laughing.

Holly laughed, too. She so wished she could have the carefree attitude Tessa had. "You know what?" she said, finishing her wine in one gulp. "You're right. I don't need a man to make my life complete, and I certainly don't need Jared. Come on. Let your rich, older sister take you out to dinner tonight. You can be my Valentine."

40

Holly and Tessa walked into the Urban Bistro at eight o'clock. They'd intended to leave earlier, but neither one of them could agree on where to go. Every suggestion of where to eat was attached to a memory— for Holly it was with either Ben or Jared, and for Tessa with the multitude of boyfriends she'd had over the past few years. They'd finally resorted to looking at an online restaurant listing. It took getting to the letter U before they could find someplace without any significance.

"Table for two please," Holly innocently asked as they walked into the crowded establishment.

"What name is your reservation under?" The woman, dressed all in black, stood at a podium and flipped through the papers attached to her clipboard without looking up.

"Oh," Holly replied, "we don't have a reservation."

The hostess stopped flipping papers, her bright red lips coming together in an odd pout, as she scanned the two girls from head to toe. "You do know it's Valentine's Day, don't you? We've been booked for months."

"We're aware of the date, thank you," Tessa responded, returning the head to toe scan. "Do you serve food at the bar?"

The woman motioned to the left with her head and called, "Next!" to the couple behind them.

"She's a friendly one," Tessa said as they walked in the direction of the packed room. "Do you want to stay or try to go somewhere else?"

"We might as well stay. I have a feeling we'd get the same story anywhere we'd go. I wasn't thinking about the whole reservation thing. Besides, we'd have to go back to our list, and I don't know how many restaurants are left after U that meet our *no connection* criteria."

"Good point. Hey, that couple at the bar is leaving. Let's grab their seats."

Tessa grasped Holly's arm and raced over, squeezing in as an older couple approached. She smiled at them and shrugged as the man gave her a dirty look. The annoyed pair huffed off and stood in the corner.

"I thought he was about to deck you. Maybe we should offer these stools to them. We can wait for something else to open up. I feel bad."

"Nonsense, they're going to get called any minute for their fancy table. We're here for the long haul. Menus please," Tessa asked when the bartender came over."

"This is a nice place," Holly noted. "Romantic. No wonder it's been booked for months. I'm surprised I've never been here."

The bartender handed them menus, and she opened hers up and gasped. "O-kay, now I know why I've never been here. So you know the part about me being the rich sister taking you out for dinner?"

"Yeah," Tessa said, still holding hers closed on her lap.

"I'm not this rich! Maybe you want a cup of soup for dinner? And some water?"

Her sister opened her menu to see what all the fuss was about. "Holy shit!" she yelled. Then covered her mouth. "Sorry. Let's go back to Mom and Dad's for dinner. We can pick up another bottle of wine on the way and scrounge around their kitchen for some grub. Do people really spend this much on food?"

"I guess," Holly said, relieved they were leaving. "Let me just use the bathroom first." She grabbed her coat.

"Good idea."

Holly noticed that the older couple were making their way over to their empty seats again, only this time the man was walking a lot faster. She chuckled and turned to leave the bar area. As they got closer to the entrance to the dining room, she stopped short. Tessa bumped into her back.

"Why'd you stop walking?" she asked.

"Sh," Holly whispered, pointing. She pulled her sister around the corner so they could both peek into the main dining room without being spotted.

"Looks like I was right about their plans for the evening," Tessa noted, watching Michelle and Ben sitting at a far table. "Apparently the plastics plant pays pretty well these days. Guess Ben was holding out on you since he never took you here."

Looking at her sister, Holly rolled her eyes. "She's probably paying for it. She's some fancy executive, remember? Ugh. Why do I keep seeing him everywhere I go?"

"Fate. I keep trying to tell you. He looks absolutely miserable."

"Wouldn't you? Anyway, let's just go to the bathroom and get out of here. The last thing I want to do is watch them have their little romantic dinner."

"She's getting up," Tessa noted. "And she's heading toward the bathroom. Now what are we going to do? I'm not in the mood to bump into Miss High and Mighty tonight."

"Me either. I guess we'll have to wait. How long can she possibly take?"

They leaned back into the wall and watched as she walked down the hallway toward the restrooms. However, Michelle didn't go into the bathroom. She pulled out her phone and typed something. Seconds later, a man appeared. He took Michelle in his arms and kissed her passionately. Holly was too shocked to move. Luckily, Tessa wasn't. She pulled out her phone and took pictures. Then grabbing Holly's arm, she proceeded to quickly walk toward them.

"This is not happening on my watch," she said.

Walking straight up to the guy, Tessa nudged him to the side.

"Hey!" Michelle shrieked. "What do you think—" She stopped suddenly, pretending to fix her hair. "Holly, Tessa, hello. This is, um, Simon Grady. He's a business associate of mine."

"Hello," Holly said, refusing to shake his outstretched hand.

"Business associate?" Tessa questioned. "So this is a business meeting then?"

Michelle nodded.

"Interesting," she noted. "Do all of your business meetings involve sucking face, or is it only the ones involving men?"

"I beg your pardon. How rude!"

"Indeed!" Tessa said, trying to imitate her uppity tone. "Does your boyfriend, Ben, know you're back here holding a private *business meeting* on *Valentine's Day*? How about you, Simon was it? I'm assuming you're here with your date as well?"

"That's really none of your business," Michelle stated.

"I'm thinking maybe we should make it our business. After all, Ben's kind of like family. Isn't that right, Holly?"

Holly stood there nodding, so appreciative Tessa was there to take control of the situation. She wished Michelle didn't intimidate the hell out of her.

"Go for it," Michelle said, laughing. "Like I'm sure he'll believe you."

"I-I have to get back to my wi ... er ... table," Simon muttered as he ran off.

"Yes, I need to be getting back as well." Turning on her heels, she began marching back to the table, appearing more confident than ever.

"Sorry I took so long, love," she said in her sickening sweet voice, with Tessa and Holly following close behind, "but you'll never guess who I ran in to."

Ben placed his napkin on the table and rose to give the sisters a hug. "So nice to see you both." He gazed at Holly with longing in his eyes before looking around. "Are you two here alone?"

Tessa smirked. "Well, we don't have dates if that's what you mean. However, we did just meet Michelle's business associate. Simon was it? I guess he decided not to join us, since that would have been awkward, don't you think, Michelle?"

"Pardon?" she said with a strange smile, as if she didn't understand the question.

Tessa pulled out her phone and continued, "Aren't these new smart phones wonderful?" she asked. "You can take great photos from so far away. Would you like to see a few I shot today?"

"Sure," Ben replied, keeping his eyes on Holly.

"Maybe another time, sweetie," Michelle said sternly, rubbing her belly.

The waitress came by with their entrees, placing them on the table.

"Of course," Tessa said. "I don't want to interrupt your lovely dinner. It was great to see the two of you again. Enjoy your Valentine's Day."

Ben reached over to Tessa a peck on the cheek. "It was great to see the two of you as well. Say hello to your parents for me." He discreetly slid his hand around Holly's waist as he kissed her cheek and whispered, "I miss you," into her ear, his warm breath sending a shiver down her spine.

She tried to calm her heartbeat. Before she could say anything, Tessa grabbed her hand and led her out of the restaurant. She suddenly remembered the scene with Michelle. "I thought you were going to show him the pictures."

Her sister pulled her over to the side of the building and typed into her phone. "I just did. I texted them to him."

"I forgot you had his number."

Tessa winked.

They watched through the window of the restaurant as Ben picked up his phone. He stared at what she assumed was the photo. He then slid his phone into his pocket and continued to eat and talk to Michelle in what appeared to be his usual calm manner.

"I don't get it," Tessa said. "Why doesn't he seem upset? Isn't this the part where he yells at Michelle and storms out of the restaurant?"

"Let's go." Holly turned her back and headed to her car, trying to blink back tears yet again.

41

"**H**ey, Holly." Dan poked his head into her classroom as he walked by. "Alex and I are grabbing a bite after work. Are you interested?"

Any other time she'd say yes. But after what she just went through last week, she was in no mood to go out. She didn't understand. Why hadn't those pictures bothered Ben?

"Sorry," she half-smiled, "I'm way behind on my lesson plans. Next time?"

"You've been saying that all week," he said, "I'm worried about you."

She glanced at the reflection coming from the hallway, bouncing off the window in her classroom. "Elaine Fairview approaching," she warned.

Dan flattened himself and hid behind her door.

"Pardon me," Elaine said, knocking as she spoke.

Holly cringed as she watched the door slam into her boss.

"Yes, Mrs. Fairview, what can I help you with?"

"I was looking for Dan. Have you seen him by chance?"

"Nope," she answered, trying to appear angelic. "I haven't. So sorry."

"Well, if you do, can you tell him I've been looking for him?"

"Yes," she added, nodding. "I most certainly will."

Elaine spun around on her heels and walked back into the hallway without so much as a good-bye or a thank you. Holly watched her turn the corner in the reflection and motioned for Dan to come out when the coast was clear. She burst into a fit of laughter.

"Thanks," he said, lowering his voice. "I owe you one. She's mad at me because I won't go along with the changes to the curriculum she's proposing. She doesn't think the sixth-graders should be learning pre-algebra in the spring. She thinks we should dumb it down for them. If you ask me, maybe *she's* the one who can't handle the material."

"Even some of my fifth-graders can handle pre-algebra," Holly said. "Hell, a few are ready for calculus!"

"I know. Every time I try to tell her that, her eyes bulge so much they look as if they might pop out of her skull. I'm honestly only avoiding her because I'm afraid she's going to have a coronary right on the spot. Well, then I'd have to fill out a bunch of accident paperwork, and you know how much I hate extra paperwork."

Holly started giggling all over again.

"It's good to see you laughing."

"Oh, I'm okay," she said. "Just in a little funk, I guess."

"Well, are you sure you don't want to go out?"

"Thanks, I appreciate the offer. I'm just—I have some stuff I need to work through on my own. I'll be fine, promise."

Holly finished up her schoolwork and headed home, retreating even further into isolation. In addition to Dan's offer, Tessa had texted her to see if she wanted to come by her apartment for a movie and some take-out. She replied with a '*thanks but no thanks.*' Even her mom tried to get her to come out of her room under the guise of looking at a new apartment she'd heard about across town that was opening up soon. It was a useless endeavor.

Holly knew in the back of her mind she was being unreasonable. Hiding in her room wouldn't make the situation with Ben go away.

Hey, we haven't talked in days. Text me.

Ava. The last time she talked to her sister was right before Valentine's Day. While Ava knew she was heartbroken over the situation with Michelle, Holly felt uncomfortable telling her about the picture. Ben was Max's cousin, and this baby was going to be part of Ava's family, whether Holly liked it or not. She didn't want to be the one responsible for creating conflict if Ben was choosing to ignore it. It was easier for her to keep quiet about the entire thing.

Sitting at her desk, she tried to grade papers, but her mind wandered to Ben. She needed to forget about him. Yes, she told him it was important for him to try to work it out with Michelle because of the baby, but everything was different now. Michelle was nothing more than a two-bit cheater, and even worse was that Ben knew it. Maybe the baby wasn't even his ... maybe all the stuff he'd been texting Tessa was just a bunch of crap. There was nothing more Holly could do. She needed to stop this nonsense and get on with her life.

She picked up her phone again.

Hi, Ava, sorry. Been super busy with work. Love and miss you. xoxo

Except—she couldn't stop thinking about him.

"Holly? Are you in there?"

"One second, Dad!"

She opened her bedroom door to see her father holding two cue sticks.

"Care to shoot a round of pool with your old man?"

She smiled. Yes, she needed to get out of her room. She'd been cooped up for far too long, and her dad was just the man she wanted to hang out with—the one man who never let her down. "Sounds great."

She felt a spring in her step as she walked down the basement stairs ... a spring that abruptly broke when she turned the corner. Her heart stopped, and then proceeded to race uncontrollably. She could barely hear her own words over the loud beat.

"What are you doing here?" she asked.

"That old garage door was giving me trouble again," her dad interjected. "Ben came over to give me a hand. He had the magic touch, too. It's good as new. I'm going to go upstairs to grab some drinks. Why don't you two start this game without me?"

"No, Dad, wait!" she called in a panic, but it was too late, her father was already up the stairs.

"I'm sorry," Ben said. "Don't be upset with him. I tried to get Tessa to invite you out, but you wouldn't bite, so she called your dad to set this up. It was the only way I could think of to see you."

"That's why Tessa invited me over? I don't understand," Holly said, sitting down on the couch.

"I really need to talk to you," he said, taking the seat next to her. He reached for her hand and smiled.

"Ben, I don't think this is a good—" she said, pulling away.

"I saw the pictures," he said, interrupting her. "Well, not at first. After you left the restaurant, I got a text from Tessa. It was just an empty screen. I kept waiting for something to load, but Michelle was giving me dirty looks, so finally I put my phone away and forgot about it."

"That explains why you just kept eating your dinner, I suppose," Holly said. "But then you saw it?"

"Yes, when I woke up the next morning, they were there. I confronted Michelle with them, and we got into a huge fight. We were having so many problems already, and I was pretty sure it wasn't going to work, but this was the last straw. I told her it was over … and that I wanted a paternity test."

He reached over for her hands again. This time she let him take them.

Letting out a long deep breath, she smiled, her eyes filling with tears. Happy tears this time. "She admitted the baby might not be yours?"

"No," he said, shaking his head. "She still said the baby was mine. But I didn't believe her. That's why I called an attorney. It seems there's a law here that requires unwed mothers to have paternity tests done—

for the birth certificate. It's a simple blood test that can be done safely any time after the first eight weeks of pregnancy. Michelle had no choice but to go through with it. The harder part was getting the other guy to do it."

"What?" Holly asked, eyes wide. "He had to get a blood test also? How did they manage that?"

"Like I said, it's required by law here. If the mother wants the baby to be eligible for certain benefits, the birth certificate needs to have a mother *and a father's* name on it. They need a blood sample from the mother and all of the potential fathers for comparison. I guess she knew more about the situation than she originally told me, because she knew exactly who should take the test—the guy in the picture. Anyway, he refused at first. Apparently, his didn't think his *wife* would be too happy about the whole thing, but you know Michelle. She can be persuasive when she wants to be. She threatened him with a court order. The results came back this morning."

"And?" Holly asked, searching Ben's eyes for some indication of an answer.

Picking Holly up and swinging her around, he yelled, "I'm a free man! And boy, do I feel like I was just let out of prison. You have no idea." He swung her around again before lowering her down to the couch. Looking her in the eyes, he traced his fingers along her cheeks, chin, nose, and ears, before finding their way to the edges of her lips. "I've missed these lips so much," he said, continuing to draw imaginary lines around them. "I've missed everything about you. Your smell, your expressions, the way your eyes sparkle. I've been so incredibly miserable every minute I've had to be away from you."

"I've missed you, too," she whispered, yearning to taste his lips with her own. "So very much." She caressed his face, curling his hair in and out of her fingers. Not wanting to wait another moment, she wrapped her hands around the back of his head, pulling him down to her waiting lips. He eagerly obliged, his kiss full of passion.

"Wait," he said, catching his breath as he pulled away. Standing up, he kept his eyes glued to hers. "I'll be right back."

"You're leaving?" she asked, propping herself up. "Where are you going?"

"I have some unfinished business," he yelled as he ran up the stairs.

Furrowing her brow, Holly sat up as she heard the front door open and close, and then open and close once more.

Within seconds, Ben was racing back down the stairs, this time carrying an enormous red cellophane wrapped heart-shaped box of candy.

"What is this?" Holly asked, laughing.

"Last week when I saw you at the Urban Bistro, I hated that Michelle was the one sitting across from me at the table and not you. When I saw you there with

Tessa and thought the two of you were there with dates, the jealousy I felt nearly killed me."

"Now you know how I've been feeling."

"I know, and I'm so sorry you had to go through that. I hope you believe me when I tell you I never stopped loving you. I despised every second I was back with Michelle, and I need for you to know I never touched her. She is nothing but a shallow, horrid woman, and I'm so mad I even let myself get in that situation. The fact you were willing to give me up for the sake of the baby made me love you even more. God, you have no idea how much I wished that baby was *our* baby. *You* are the woman I love and adore. You are the woman I will *always* love and adore." He shifted the heart to the other hand. "Ten pounds of chocolate gets heavy after a while," he said, laughing, "but I wanted one pound for every year we were apart. And now that we're together, I can finally ask you. Holly Haines, will you be my Valentine?"

The church sat empty on the morning of September fifth. There would be no guests hurrying to take their seats as soft music played in the background, nor a nervous groom standing at the altar anxiously waiting for his bride to appear through the double doors that seemed so far away. It was a shame, actually, as Tessa had planned everything for her wedding down to the last detail. Included on the list of cancelled items were the string quartet set to play Pachelbel and Wagner as she and her bridal party walked down the aisle, the florist order of white roses and daises, and of course, the three-tiered wedding cake with the bride and groom perched on top, ready to start their happily ever after.

She and Scott had been dating ever since they met in English class the fall of their senior year at Forest Hills University. He was the handsome, popular football star, and she was getting ready for her dream job as the director in the theater school's production of *West Side Story*. Neither of them understood the assignment for the required history class they'd both put off taking until their final year. Perhaps it was coincidence, or perhaps it was fate, but they found themselves waiting outside of Professor Sutter's office at the same time to ask for help. They decided to join forces and work together. Before they knew it, they were a couple.

The pregnancy wasn't planned. Scott did what he felt was the right thing to do and proposed a week before graduation, promising to love and cherish Tessa and the baby for all of eternity. Of course, she said yes. He was her soul mate. The man she was destined to be with forever and always.

They planned to get married in early September. She'd always dreamt of a beautiful winter wedding, but the timing wouldn't work, and she didn't want to wait. If she didn't have her almost perfect white wedding now, she knew it might never happen. A late summer wedding would have to do.

As her belly swelled, so did the arguments, followed by hostility and resentment from her soon to be husband. She rationalized he was just nervous about becoming a father. They'd talked several times about having children when they were dating, and both agreed they wanted a family ... later. Neither had been prepared to welcome a baby this soon. While Tessa was looking forward to the birth of their child, Scott was still having trouble adjusting.

Her family was so focused on all of the excitement going on around them, they didn't notice the trouble brewing. Besides planning for the upcoming wedding and birth for Tessa, her other sister, Holly, had married her fiancé, Ben, only a few months earlier. Their wedding was spectacular—a dream come true for both of them. Then, there was Ava. She and her husband, Max, had recently moved back to the East Coast after having given birth to their second child, Logan. Nobody really saw the end coming, not even Tessa.

In August, two weeks before they were set to walk down the aisle, Scott called off the wedding and moved out of state without saying good-bye or leaving a forwarding address. She attempted to contact his family, but they wouldn't speak to her. She wasn't surprised. They'd wanted Scott and her to put the baby up for adoption from the moment they'd found out about the pregnancy, implying the entire *incident* was a mistake. It was no wonder he got cold feet and ran off.

On Thanksgiving Day, Sophie Rose Haines entered the world. Scott never once called to ask about his daughter.

Three Years Later

"Tessa!" Mr. Abbott bellowed from his office without getting up. "Tessa!"

She quickly put the phone on hold. The fact that she'd been waiting for fifteen minutes to speak with the nurse at her daughter's pediatrician's office was irrelevant. Her boss had made it quite clear on more than one occasion that work came first. Standing up, she straightened her blouse and steadied herself before walking one door over to face the wrath of the man who signed her paycheck.

"Yes, sir," she said, turning the corners of her lips up into a forced grin. Taking a seat in the chair opposite her boss' desk, she braced herself for the inevitable attack.

He slammed the binder down on his desk. "Your projections are off. The return on investment doesn't match the statements, and the interest calculations on the bonds are all wrong. I'm meeting with the client first thing in the morning. I can't present this to him. It's crap! Nicholas Schilling is a multi-millionaire. He pays us a lot of money to get this right ... money I use to pay you. Every time you get this wrong, you're wasting that money."

"Sir, I ran the numbers several times. They—"

"I'm telling you, they're off." Picking up the binder, he held it out as his beady eyes bore through her. "Are you going to sit there and argue? Because one of us is wrong, and it's not me."

There was no use trying to explain. Red would always be blue to him. *Always.*

"Yes, sir."

"These reports need to be completely re-done. All of them. Looks like you'll be working late." He sneered as she took the thick folder out of his hands.

Rising to her feet without another word, she quickly walked out of his office, not giving him the satisfaction of seeing the tears well up in her eyes. *Damn him.* She rushed back to her own office and picked the phone back up. The call had been disconnected. No matter, she wouldn't have time to bring Sophie to the doctor after work anyway. This job truly sucked. Well, not the job itself, but the people she had to work with ... make that person.

Her parents told her she was ridiculous when she announced she wanted to be a theater production major in college. *You'll never be able to make a living doing that.* They were right.

After Scott left and Sophie was born, Tessa moved back in with her parents. She cared for Sophie during the day, while her parents took over at night so she could work as an assistant director at the local theater. She loved the job *and* the people, but barely made enough money to pay her portion of the food bill.

At the same time, her father had just retired, and her parents were looking to sell their house. Initially, when they thought all three of their daughters were to be married off and settled, they had put a deposit down on a condo a few towns over. The place was perfect for them—a fifty-five and older community with lots of activities. Unfortunately for Tessa, it meant she would need to find a new place to live, as her parents would now be in a tiny home that didn't allow young residents. It also meant she was stuck looking for alternative childcare. While her parents would still be close enough to see their grandkids regularly, the hour plus commute would make them too far to be her daily sitter. With rent and daycare expenses now looming, she had no choice but to give up her theater job.

Thankfully, her father had an old college friend, Bruce, a local accountant and financial planner, who was looking for some office help. The pay was decent, and there was a good yet inexpensive daycare close by. She was able to move out of her parents' house before it sold and into her own tiny apartment. Bruce was a kind man who taught Tessa about the business. She found it interesting and learned the ropes quickly. After a year, Bruce, like her parents, decided he was also ready to retire. He sold the business to one of his competitors: Steven Abbott. Mr. Abbott, as he insisted on being called, agreed to keep her on as part of the deal. Unlike Bruce, however, her new boss was not a kind man. He was ruthless ... and heartless.

Tessa constantly had her eyes out for another job. She worried, though. This one was close to Sophie's daycare, gave her basic medical insurance, and covered her rent. And who's to say her next boss would be any better? Although, it was highly unlikely she'd get stuck with someone worse. She sent out inquiries on a weekly basis with no luck. It looked like she was stuck with Mr. Abbott whether she wanted to be or not.

She began to dial the telephone again.

"Pick up, please, pick up," she whispered just as she heard the familiar *"Hello?"*

"Hi, it's Tessa. I need your help."

Karen Pokras writes adult contemporary and middle grade fiction under the names Karen Pokras and Karen Pokras Toz. Her books have won several awards including two Readers' Favorite Book Awards, the Grand Prize in the Purple Dragonfly Book Awards, as well as placing first for two Global E-Book Awards for Pre-Teen Literature. A native of Connecticut, Karen now lives outside of Philadelphia with her family. For more information, visit www.karenpokras.com and www.karentoz.com

I'm so glad I was able to continue this series for you. Holly's story was a challenging one to write, and this book wouldn't be what it is without the input of some amazing people: Alicia Marietta, Kathie Juliano, Jane Anne Linsdell, editor Melissa Ringsted of There For You Editing, and author Kristy K. James. I'd also like to give a special thank you to the wonderful team at Najla Qamber Designs for creating my beautiful cover: designer Najla Qamber, models Courtney Boyett and Willis Totten, and photographer Casey Totten.

And to my readers— Thank you for reading my stories! As always, your support means everything to me. Feel free to drop me a line - **I love hearing from you!**

karenpokrasauthor@gmail.com

Other Books By Karen Pokras

Whispered Wishes Series:
Book 1: Ava's Wishes
Book 2: Holly's Wishes
Book 3: Tessa's Wishes
Book 4: Woven Wishes
Merry Wishes: A Whispered Wishes Novella

Chasing Invisible (Karen Pokras Toz)

Books for Children 7-12 (Karen Pokras Toz)
Nate Rocks the World
Nate Rocks the Boat
Nate Rocks the School
Nate Rocks the City
Millicent Marie Is Not My Name
Pie and Other Brilliant Idea